Janna MacGregor
Kisses by Candlelight
Romantic Regency Shorts

Praise for Janna MacGregor

"Mesmerizing! Janna MacGregor pens enchanting characters and passionate romance that offers the perfect escape." —— *New York Times* bestseller Lorraine Heath

"If ... looking for something new with Austen's spirit, humor, and dashing heroes, they can't do better than MacGregor."— *Entertainment Weekly*

"Janna MacGregor dazzles her readers with sexy stories that are also endearingly tender. Her characters tug at your heart-strings and make you sad to turn the last page." —— *New York Times* bestseller Eloisa James

"Janna MacGregor's stories positively sparkle. Filled with heart, humor, and passion, she is an absolute must read!" —— *USA Today* bestselling author Christi Caldwell

Copyright © 2023 by Janna MacGregor

All Rights Reserved. Except as permitted under the U.S. Copyright Act of 1976, no part of this publication may be reproduced, distributed, or transmitted in any form or by any means, or stored in a database or retrieval system without prior written permission from the author.

This book is a work of fiction. Names, characters, places, and incidents are the product of the author's imagination or are use facetiously. Any resemblance to actual events, locales, or persons, living or dead is coincidental.

NO AI TRAINING: Without in any way limiting the author's exclusive rights under copyright, any use of this publication to "train" generative artificial intelligence (AI) technologies to generate text is expressly prohibited. The author reserves all rights to license uses of this work for generative AI training and development of machine learning language models.

Kisses by Candlelight/Janna MacGregor

1. Regency Romance 2. Romance. 3. Christmas Romance 4. Holiday Romance

Cover design by Forever After Romance Designs

About the Book

The Earl's Christmas Bride

Cameron Dunmore, the Earl of Queensgrace, is determined to win the hand of his true love, Miss Julia Lawson. Julia never forgot Cameron, but she won't abandon her family, even if she must sacrifice her own happiness. When a Christmas angel in the guise of Julia's little brother brings these stubborn lovebirds together, only Cam and Julia can decide if Christmas wedding bells are in their future.

Red Ribbons and Rogues

Every year, Miss Eve Marchant's brother, Lord Simon Marchant, and his wife, Lady Corinne Marchant, host a huge Christmas Eve party for their houseguests at the viscount's ancestral estate. When Eve sees the man of her dreams kiss another woman under the mistletoe, she's convinced this is the worst holiday ever. But, with a little bit of holiday magic, perhaps her worst day turns into a dream come true.

Never Enough Mistletoe Kisses

ABOUT THE BOOK

Miss Clarissa Bickham can barely tolerate all the good cheer
present at her grandfather's holiday party. Is it any wonder when everyone seems to be celebrating with their *special someone* except Clarissa? Tonight marked the evening when she and her beloved Ethan Thorton were to be married, but Ethan has been away on a special military mission to France for over six months. Clarissa hasn't heard a word from him. When her spry grandfather sends her on a special errand, Clarissa finds a surprise waiting.

Will this Christmas finally find her and Ethan pledging their troth to one another?

Kissing Boughs and Pampered Pugs

Though Jane Hosmer has her adorable pug, Poppy, beside her this holiday season, Jane can't help but feel a little melancholy. It's been three long and lonely years since she last saw her special someone, Heath Ladylove. Will this be the fourth Christmas in a row without Heath or, will Poppy somehow create a Christmas miracle?

**Sign up for Janna's newsletter at
https://www.jannamacgregor.com**

Contents

The Earl's Christmas Bride	ix
Chapter 1	1
Chapter 2	8
Chapter 3	13
Chapter 4	20
Chapter 5	26
Chapter 6	36
Chapter 7	41
Red Ribbons and Rogues	49
Red Ribbons and Rogues	51
Never Enough Mistletoe Kisses	57
Never Enough Mistletoe Kisses	59
Kissing Boughs and Pampered Pugs	67
Kissing Boughs and Pampered Pugs	69
Other Books by Janna MacGregor	79
Under the Marquess's Mistletoe	81
The Duchess of Drury Lane	89

The Earl's Christmas Bride

A CAVENSHAM HEIRESSES NOVELLA

One

The nobs, fobs, and fops careened around Cameron Dunmore, the Earl of Queensgrace, like spinning tops set loose on the streets of London. Hither and thither, grown men raced from shop to shop on Bond Street, packages overflowing from their arms. Since Scotland really didn't celebrate Christmas, such a sight should have been highly entertaining.

However, Cam ignored the bustle as he'd found what he was looking for, and she was definitely more intriguing than spinning tops. He leaned close to the boy selling roasted chestnuts from the small cart beside him. "See that lass yonder?"

The boy scrunched his nose then followed Cam's pointed finger. "Yes, m' lord." The boy's gaze jerked back to Cam. "You are a lord, ain' you?"

Cam nodded gently. "Scottish."

The boy nodded once in answer as if that one word explained everything, then rubbed his hands over the fire where he roasted his chestnuts. He blew out a breath, and a wave of white steam escaped.

"Now, I have a job for you." Cam pulled out a brand-new

guinea and held it between his thumb and forefinger. "This is yours if you approach that bonnie lass and give her a bag of chestnuts." Magically, he pulled another from his cuff. "They're both yours if you give her the nuts and this." Gently, he reached into his waistcoat pocket and retrieved a rose posy, somewhat smashed but still vibrant in color.

The boy tilted his head and regarded him. With fingerless gloves on his hands, he nimbly took the posy, then straightened the flowers and tidied the lace ribbon holding the small bouquet together. Satisfied with his work, he tipped his hat to Cam. "I'll have 'er eatin' out of m' hand. Watch m' cart." Without waiting for a reply, he set off to give the tokens to the lovely lady not ten paces away.

Cam's gut tightened. He'd have approached her himself, but after the way he'd made a mash of proposing to her, he didn't want to cause her further embarrassment. He'd told her sister, Miss March Lawson, that he'd planned to come the next day and propose, but his only sister, Lara, had summoned him immediately.

Her husband of twelve years, Ewan MacFarland, had died of a lung infection. Beside herself with no one except Cam to turn to, Lara had begged for him to return to Edinburgh. Stupidly, Cam had sent a note to his one true love's sister, but not to her. He blinked and said a little prayer.

Father, give me another chance. It's all I'll ever ask for this Christmastide.

His hands tightened into fists by his sides as the boy spoke to Miss Julia Lawson, the fairest lass in all the kingdom. Even London, the most jaded town in all the British Isles, proclaimed her the bonniest lass of all. Even *The Midnight Cryer,* the vilest gossip rag ever to have been printed, had crowned her a diamond of the first water.

Cam had never understood the expression, but he knew it was something rare and beautiful—just like her. With eyes bluer than sapphires and hair that would rival the most brilliant sun, she stood at an angle that allowed him to gaze his fill.

He tried to shake the trepidation that felt like a dead weight on his shoulders. That Julia would welcome him with open arms was highly doubtful. After he'd raced back from Scotland, he'd called upon her twice at McCalpin House. Always she'd been "out" and unavailable. Both times when Cam had left, he'd felt as if someone was watching him. He'd always wondered if it was her, or just his wishful imagination. But today he'd found her and wouldn't let her go without first explaining himself. He could only hope that she'd not cut him directly and walk out of his life forever.

❄

"Miss, I have somethin' for ye." The small boy who sold chestnuts on the street corner had left his post and stood before Julia. His big brown eyes and soft brown curls could melt an iceberg in the Arctic Sea. He handed her a bag of still-warm chestnuts, and a rather smashed but brilliant posy made up of red roses, her favorite. The roses reminded her of the bouquet that arrived on her doorstep every week.

"Oh, how thoughtful." She opened her reticule to retrieve a coin for payment. "Thank you. How did you know that I was hungry?"

Though he was only ten years old, her brother, Lord Bennett Lawson had accompanied her on the shopping trip for a few presents for their sisters and brothers-in-law. She had the perfect present, a new chess set, picked out for him, but she couldn't buy it with him here.

Bennett bent over the bag and examined the treasures

inside. With an exaggerated inhale he declared, "Amazing that the vendors now offer curb service."

The boy selling chestnuts shook his head slightly as if unamused with her brother's quip. "It's from his lordship over thar." The boy jabbed a thumb behind his shoulder.

When Julia smiled then glanced to see who'd sent such delightful gifts, she'd half expected one of her sisters and their husbands to be the responsible party.

She definitely didn't expect to find *him* staring at her. From across the street, his gray eyes sparkled with a heat designed to melt away any remaining anger she possessed. His black greatcoat and beaver hat emphasized his towering height. The wind teased the long length of his chestnut-colored hair that brushed his shoulders. Why had he let it grow so long? He'd always been meticulous with his appearance, but truthfully, it only enhanced his masculine looks. Her heart always skipped a beat when she gazed at his sharply angled cheeks and handsome visage. Even with a slight bend on the bridge of his nose, he was striking. Ever since he'd told her that he'd broken it as a boy when his horse shied from making a jump, she'd been enthralled with him.

She pursed her lips. She didn't have time to waste another second with thoughts of Cameron Dunmore, the Earl of Queensgrace—the man who'd jilted her even before he'd asked her to marry him.

"Will he ever leave you alone, Jules?" Bennett asked with his green eyes trained on Queensgrace. "Don't worry. I'll handle this man-to-man."

Julia shot her hand out and grabbed Bennett by the arm stopping him from crossing the street. Unfortunately, it did little to tame the anger that had his nostrils flaring. "I appreciate what you're doing, but allow me to discourage Lord—"

"Lord Lawson." The earl stood before them, then elegantly nodded his greeting.

In retaliation, the young viscount lifted his chin another inch in the air.

Ignoring her brother's rebuff, Lord Queensgrace settled his brilliant gaze on hers. "Miss Lawson, may I say that you are a ray of warm sunshine from the heavens on this cold, dreary London morning." The earl took her hand and gently squeezed it in greeting, then executed a perfect bow.

Bennett rolled his eyes.

The earl witnessed her brother's dramatic gesture and laughed in response. The rich baritone wrapped around her like a heated blanket.

Which was appropriate as fire bludgeoned her cheeks. *Bother it all.* She didn't want any part of his six-foot three-inch lean muscular body to have an effect on her. Yet here she stood on a London street corner blushing like a school girl with her first crush—*never mind that he was her one and only crush*. At first sight, she'd fallen in love with him. She'd have followed him to the ends of the earth until he'd crushed her with a broken promise of marriage.

Discreetly, the earl slipped something into the boy's hand, and the little vendor skipped back to his cart. The earl's gaze strayed to his boots as if struggling to find something to say. He rocked back on his heels.

"Julia—"

"Cam—"

They both chuckled awkwardly at speaking over the other. But when their gazes caught, the familiar magical electricity that always coursed through her body when he was near, laid claim over her. Then their silence turned from tongue-tied to familiar. It was more like an unspoken conversation between them.

His gray eyes softened. *I missed you.*

And I you. Hot tears gathered in her eyes. *Every day since you left me.*

Don't cry, sweetheart. Give me another chance.

"Julia, we should leave." Bennett tugged his gloves tightly as he waited for her to lead the way.

"One moment, Bennett." To encourage her tears to evaporate, she turned her head into the biting December wind. It was pure madness to even consider allowing him back into her heart and into her life after he'd hurt her so.

The earl reached into his waistcoat pocket and withdrew a pristine embroidered handkerchief. Instead of blotting her eyes, she held it to her nose and inhaled. His fragrance of fresh cedar and sandalwood filled her lungs. It reminded her of the season and all those nights when he'd danced with her at the various *ton* events, practically declaring in front of London society that she was his.

She held his scent as long as she could. Another simple pleasure she'd missed in her life.

If she continued in such a manner, she'd make herself sick with grief. She was long past shedding tears and losing sleep over this man. "It's good to see you, Queensgrace. I wish you a happy Christmastide."

She clutched the handkerchief tight while she slipped her other hand through Bennett's fingers. In response, he opened his mouth to protest such an act. She could recite his protest from memory since she'd heard it so many times. He was a man and didn't need his sisters to look after him. She squeezed his hand with hers.

"Please, Bennett." She lowered her voice to a whisper. "It's not for you, but for me. I *need* to hold your hand." She'd steal whatever strength she could from his warmth.

"Wait. Please." Queensgrace took a step nearer decreasing the distance between them. His tall and broad physique blocked the north wind's assault. "Please, Julia…Jules. I beg of you."

Her gaze snapped to his. Her family's chosen nickname for

Julia resonated like an invitation to sin when his deep heavy voice whispered her name. But the pleading in his words caught her by surprise.

"I'll get down on my hands and knees if that's what it'll take. Let me at least have a chance to explain what happened."

She nodded once while still squeezing Bennett's hand. "Come tomorrow at nine."

It was Christmastide, and even Scottish louts, who were too handsome for their own good, deserved a little goodwill and glad tidings.

Two

The next morning, Julia and Bennett sat in the small breakfast room. Though the bold navy and red furnishings normally captured her attention, all Julia could do was stare out the window. Each tick from the longcase clock brought her closer to her meeting with Cameron.

Just seeing him after these six long months brought a plethora of emotions to the surface. Pleasure, pain, joy, and doubt mixed together in a perfect recipe for misery. For icing on the cake, her stomach had twisted into knots that even the most experienced sailor could never untangle.

Bennett leaned back in his chair and stroked the silky black fur of his cat, Maximus. Since the rest of family were out all day, Julia allowed Maximus the run of the dining room. When they lived at their ancestral seat of Lawson Abbey in Leyton, Maximus always found a way to join the family for meals. But when her oldest sister, March Lawson, had married the Marquess of McCalpin, the entire family, including her, their other sister Faith, and Bennett, had joined them. Julia closed her eyes and sighed.

Growing up at the Abbey was a fond memory. In their hometown of Leyton, she never had to worry with gossip or innuendos. But London had taught her how plain meanness and vile rumors could ooze from society—particularly whenever they saw her. Six long months ago, everyone within the *ton* along with her two sisters, March and Faith, thought Julia would marry Cameron.

But then Cameron had disappeared like a ghost into a wall leaving Julia the one left with the carnage. The gossip rag, *The Midnight Cryer*, repeatedly said she'd been jilted. Within a week, she'd received a houseful of flowers from Cameron begging her forgiveness, but he'd never called upon her. A month later he sent another note explaining his sister had been ill. Because her complete recovery was questionable, he thought it unfair to keep Julia waiting for his return. Though they weren't officially betrothed, Cam released her from any promises that existed between them. He'd ended the note with a heartfelt wish that she find happiness in her life.

Julia had been devastated when she received his message. She'd always wondered if it was some excuse to hide the fact that he didn't want her anymore. But starting two months ago, beautiful red rose bouquets were delivered every week with a card simply signed, "Queensgrace."

Days then weeks passed by and eventually, her sister Faith had married the love of her life, Dr. Mark Kennett, a successful London physician. Both March and Faith had found the true loves of their lives while Julia had just mildewed like a piece of stale bread. But truth be told, Julia was ecstatic that her sisters had married such fine men. Secretly, she'd always held out hope there was a marvelous man for her to take as a husband.

Yet because of Cameron, damage had been done. Her reputation for one. After Cameron had left, no other suitor feigned any interest in her, the last unmarried Lawson sister. Which made it all the more understandable that she was angry with him. But if she was honest with herself, yesterday after she saw him, the anger that had festered for months slowly started to whither.

Her fickle heart.

"Since I'm the man of the house, I'll not allow that vagabond to upset you any further." Bennett straightened the simple knot of his cravat, then pulled down his waistcoat as if he'd not tolerate any nonsense from the earl.

"You're the man of the house because the marquess is out with March." She reached out and petted Maximus. The black cat slowly blinked his gold eyes, then rewarded her with a purr.

"You should have told March and McCalpin that Queensgrace would call this morning."

"I did." Julia slowly shook her head. "However, I need to talk to him by myself."

"Let me deal with him." Her ten-year-old brother announced. "I'll have him thrown out quicker than Maximus can catch a mouse."

She shouldn't be surprised at Bennett's reaction. He'd inherited their father's viscountcy when he was less than a year old. Every day, he became more and more comfortable in that role. Still, it amazed her that her little brother had turned into a very proper and very protective young man who would shield her at any cost.

"Bennett, what would I do without you?" Truly, Julia loved her little brother with all her heart. Though he irritated her at times, he was her *only* brother. She glanced around at the opulence of the room, but her gaze froze at the window. It looked like a blizzard had hit Mayfair. "Look it's snowing."

At the word "snow," Bennett put Maximus down then rushed to the window, proving he was still a boy interested in the season's delights.

"*Snow.*" Bennett motioned her forward. "Just look at it, Jules!"

She joined Bennett at the window and gazed at the sparkling blanket of white before them. Such a snowfall was rare in London, but this would guarantee a white Christmas since it was only three days away.

The clock struck half past the hour indicating that Cameron was late. A round of goosebumps prickled her skin like thousands of tiny icicle shards pelting her. She rubbed her hands on the upper part of her arms to keep the cold away. But it still didn't lessen the fear that he wouldn't come.

No matter what, this was the last chance she'd give him. She exhaled. Was she really considering giving him another chance? She shook her head to clear such thoughts.

She glanced down at Bennett fully expecting him to still be inspecting the snow. Instead, her brother silently studied his shoe. "Julia?"

"Hmm?" A thick black curl had fallen across his forehead. With her fingers, she gently combed it back in place.

"Don't marry him," Bennett said softly. "I don't want to lose you, too."

She leaned closer until they were almost eye level. "What do mean 'lose me'?"

"Now that March and Faith are married, it's just you and me. You're the one who always quizzes me on my lessons. You correct my grammar and spelling." His cheeks blossomed into a fiery red. "You read to me."

"We read together," she added.

Discreetly, he nodded in answer. "You make time for me."

Really, this was so unlike Bennett to feel this insecure. Normally, he was the one who gave the orders to his three sisters when the siblings all gathered together.

"You and I are all that's left of the Lawson family." His voice cracked on the last two words which caused another bout of red cheeks. "He'll take you to Scotland, and I'll never see you. You're the only one I have left."

Those softly spoken words hit her square in the stomach and gutted her. She slowly blinked as she struggled for equilibrium.

When she'd been a little girl, Julia had felt the same fear when their parents had died. After suffering such a devastating loss, her place in the world had become untethered like an unmoored boat drifting aimlessly without the security of an anchor. Julia hadn't let her oldest sister, March, or her other sister, Faith, out of her sight for months. How could she even allow her darling brother to suffer the same?

She pulled him into her embrace and pressed a kiss on top of his head. His arms clenched her waist with a grip that defied his age.

"Bennett, look at me." She pulled away and tilted his chin until their gazes met. His eyes glistened with emotion, and her heart lurched at the sight. "The earl hasn't asked me to marry him. Don't worry about things that haven't happened. As long as you need me, I'll be by your side. Understand?"

He nodded once.

A footman cleared his throat. "Miss Lawson, the Earl of Queensgrace is calling. I put him in the front sitting room. Are you receiving?"

"Yes, I'll see him." She squeezed Bennett once more, then slowly released her hold. Instead of looking at her, he studied the falling snow outside. But she saw the lone tear that cascaded down his cheek.

He quickly dashed it away. "I'm going outside."

"After I finish with Queensgrace, I'll join you."

"I'd like that," he said softly, then quickly ran from the room.

Taking her heart with him.

Three

Cam stared at the falling snow outside the window that looked over the private courtyard at McCalpin House. Such a serene sight did little to calm his racing heartbeat that pounded in time with each movement of the second hand on his pocket watch. Each tick reminded him that he had to make the most of this chance to win Julia's hand.

"Hello, Cam."

Such a mellifluous sound instantly slowed the battering inside his chest. He turned and found a vision before him that would have made angels sing praise to the heavens.

His Julia.

All five feet five inches of her regally stood before him. Dressed in an azure brocade gown with a silver lace overlay, she was a vision of beauty.

God, how he'd missed her. When he'd left to attend his sister at the sudden death of her husband, he'd left his heart in her possession. Did she have any idea the power she held over him? Her incomparable beauty could make a man mute. But he couldn't let it overshadow what he'd come to accomplish today. He'd not leave without her agreeing to allow him another chance. Nor would he leave without giving her the proper kiss he'd meant to give her before he left.

"Julia—" His traitorous throat thickened. In an attempt to tame the riot of emotions, he cleared his voice.

Before he could say another word, she closed the distance between them.

With an elegant ease that betrayed the turmoil running amok through him, he took her hand and brought it to his lips. The warmth of her skin could soothe the most jaded of beasts, and he allowed his lips to linger and savor the softness that resided there.

"Would you care to sit, or will your visit be short?" she asked serenely. The blue of her eyes sparkled, and a smile tugged at her lips.

Her inner imp was in rare form today. She knew *bloody* well that he wanted to spend every moment of his life with her starting now, and if she didn't, she soon would. "My visit will be as long as necessary to convince you to give me a second chance at wooing you, lass."

The smile on her face could light the entire end of East London with its brilliance. "Ah well, then I don't think I have enough refreshments to serve you forever."

"Refreshments might only be a nuisance for what I have planned." Unable to hold his mirth at her antics inside, he laughed. Her eyes widened. But the feigned shock didn't fool him as her gaze grew even brighter.

"Why is that?" She walked to a Louis XV settee, then sat.

He settled beside her, then angled his body so he could see every glorious inch of her. "Because I plan to kiss you until you forgive me." He leaned closer until an inch separated their lips.

Her mouth formed a perfect and endearing "o." Her gentle breath brushed his cheek. He took a deep breath, then slowly released it to keep from possessing her on the sofa that very instant. Every blond hair, eyelash, and inch of her perfect skin was his, and he'd do his damnedest to convince her of it.

"Julia, I've thought of this moment every single day since I left London." Gently, he took her hands in his. "I've thought of *you* every hour and minute of the day. I've dreamt of *you* every night."

One perfect eyebrow arched in disbelief, but she didn't release his hand which gave him hope.

"It wasn't fear of marriage or unwanted gossip that kept me from coming to ask for your hand last May." He bit the side of his cheek and hoped he'd find the words to convince her. "You must know that I'd have never left you to fend on your own had I known what those heathens at *The Midnight Cryer* were capable of printing about you and me."

Her face remained frozen, and she didn't offer a word.

"My heart was ripped in two by what they said I'd done to you. I never left you, lass."

"Yes, you did," she answered curtly. "For over six *long* months. Besides, your last letter released me from a betrothal that never existed."

"No." He shook his head. "Never. Do you know why?"

She bit one adorable lip in answer.

Unable to resist, he brushed his thumb across her plush lower lip. "Because I left my heart with you."

She slowly blinked her eyes and took a ragged breath. His Julia was strong, but she was hurting now. He hated to cause her pain, but as his dear mother had always said, *you must lance the wound before it can heal.*

"Then why didn't you come back for me?" she asked softly. "Why didn't you at least write more than the note that your sister was ill and might never recover? If I meant that much to you...was it just an excuse?"

"No, sweetheart." He ran a hand through his hair as he

struggled to explain his actions. How to share the fact his sister had gone practically stark-raving mad after her husband had died? He'd never felt so alone or so helpless when he'd returned home to Edinburgh.

"It's true my notes were vague, but it wasn't something I could write about. In my missives, I told you part of the story but not all." Cam rested his elbows on his legs and studied his hands. He'd always been strong with brawny muscles and stamina, but Lara had taught him that physical strength meant nothing if you didn't have emotional fortitude. "After my sister's husband died, she called me home. What I found there would have made even a witch's toes curl."

Julia put one delicate hand over his. "If you're not comfortable sharing, I understand."

"No, I'll hide nothing from you." He placed his other hand atop hers. His were so much larger than hers, but the warmth of her skin beckoned him to tell her everything. "Lara had always put her family first. Her husband and her sons were everything in the world to her. I had always thought of her as the glue that held the family together. She'd always been able to handle anything that life could throw her way. When Ewan died that hadn't been the case—not when she left her two small boys alone to care for themselves when she disappeared."

"What happened?" Julia's voice had softened, but her eyes warmed with an unmistakable empathy at his words. "Where did she go?"

"I don't know. When I went to their home, I found my nephews alone, hungry, and dirty. She'd been gone for at least a week. I took Kinnon and Tavis to my estate. Once they were safe and sound, I assigned my housekeeper to look after them while I rode over practically every stream and crag in the highlands to find their mother. This went on for weeks. I couldn't trust that what I wrote to you wouldn't fall into the wrong hands." He shook his head gently as the feelings of helplessness and agony threatened to take his words. "I found her alone in a rundown shack not far from Edinburgh. I thought she'd be ruined if anyone found out about her disappearance." He swallowed the grip of emotion that held tight. "I didn't want any of it to taint you." He huffed a feigned laugh. "But I only put you in a worse situation."

"Oh, Cam. I'm so sorry," she said gently. "That must have been horrible for her sons...and for you. Where are Lara and the boys now?"

"I brought them with me to London. I couldn't leave them alone, but I couldn't stay in Scotland with you here."

She contemplated him with a depth that cut straight through him. In that instant, she saw all his faults and fears, and the truth hit him square in the chest. She'd never judge him or his sister. "I'm not certain I can find the words, but I hope you'll forgive me."

"Of course." A sad smile tugged at her lips. "I'd like to meet Lara. I'd welcome her as a friend and so would my family. And of course, your nephews."

"They'd be delighted, I'm sure. She's better now, but I can't leave her alone." Cam nodded. "Perhaps we can share a special Christmas celebration for all of us?"

An adorable expression of befuddlement crossed her face. "I didn't think Scots celebrated Christmas the way the English do."

"My mother was English and brought all the lovely traditions with her. Mince pies, mulled wine." His voice deepened as the urge to take her in his arms became overpowering. "Of course, the Scots brought the Yule log and mistletoe for sweet passionate kisses."

A soothing silence descended around them wrapping them in the safety of its comfort. A log fell on the fire, and her eyes brightened. It was the perfect timing to bring out the small gift he'd brought her. Truthfully, it was as much for him as for her, but it would bring her pleasure, or his name wasn't Cameron Dunmore. He reached into his morning coat pocket and pulled out the mistletoe posy tied with the ribbon she'd given him last spring as a token of her affection.

"Cam...you kept my ribbon?" she asked incredulously. Her eyes flashed as if truly happy making her even more beautiful.

"Next to my heart this entire time." He held the posy above her head and leaned close until no more than an inch separated them.

Her lips parted slightly, and he took that as a blessed sign from heaven that this Christmas celebration would be one forever engraved upon his heart.

He leaned until his mouth touched hers. The supple warmth from her lips was ambrosia, and he gently rubbed his against hers until the sweetest moan escaped her. Still holding the mistletoe, he wrapped her in his embrace and brought her close until her softness melded with his hardness. A perfect fit that he'd never tire of. Nor would he ever tire of her kisses. They had so much lost time to make up for. With his tongue, he traced the crease of her lips, begging for entry into her sweet mouth. With a soft breath she sighed, and he deepened the kiss.

"*Julia.*" A curt voice called from behind them.

Cam softly groaned before slowly pulling away. The desire in her eyes and the slight swelling of her lips from their kiss made him want to throw the intruder out so they could continue losing themselves in each other's arms.

"Queensgrace, I'll have you take your hands off my sister."

"Bennett, stop," she protested. "The earl is—"

"Mauling you," her little brother declared as he approached.

A perfect crimson blush colored her cheeks reminding

Cam of the hot house roses he'd ordered for her to be delivered today. Reluctantly, he let her go and turned to face her irate brother. Though the boy only came to his chest, his demeanor indicated the young viscount had the anger of a man. Frankly, Cam couldn't fault him. If it was his sister who was being kissed like there was no tomorrow, he'd object too.

"Lawson, I apologize for getting carried away. But I can assure you that I have the best intentions here." Cam extended his hand for a shake man-to-man. "I want to marry your sister."

"You pig." The grimace on the boy's face was pure disgust. "Never in a million years will I allow that."

Julia seemed to come out of the sensual fog they'd created together. "Bennett, apologize to his lordship this instant," she demanded.

"That was ill-mannered of me. I apologize," he murmured. The young viscount's cheeks turned a color reminiscent of holly berries.

"Lovely." Julia's exuberant smile was a little too bright. "Then let's all go for a walk in the snow."

"No," Bennett declared.

Cam bit his lip so he wouldn't respond to the young lord's outburst. "Miss Lawson, perhaps another time."

Julia's brow creased. "Perhaps another time?"

Cam nodded. "May I stop by tomorrow?"

"Could you come this afternoon? I think the sooner we finish our discussion, the better."

An excellent sign that she wanted him back so quickly. "I agree."

"Come for tea?" she asked.

"It would be my pleasure," Cam said softly while ignoring the young viscount's look of outrage.

Four

That afternoon, Julia inspected the front salon and found it perfectly situated for the tea she would host. She plumped the red silk pillows that adorned the deep green sofas, then counted the plates, cups, and saucers in the McCalpin china. Pleased with the festive look of the room, she walked to the side table where another massive arrangement of red roses accompanied by boughs of holly stood guard in a silver vase. She inhaled the sweet fragrance and instantly, all thoughts turned to Cam.

Her heart skipped a beat or two. Cam had made his intentions clear—he was once again her suitor. Secretly, she was thrilled that he was pursuing her so vigorously. If she'd only had to be concerned with herself, then her decision would be easy. But she'd not allow Bennett to feel discarded or ignored. Her brother was too precious to her.

But so was Cam. Though she'd been angry at him when she first saw him, once he'd explained his reasons for being vague in his letters because of his sister's disappearance, she'd been able to forgive him. Life was too short to hold such anger.

When he'd held her arms and kissed her, it'd been heaven. She realized her decision to let go of her anger was the right one. Their morning kiss had set a fire inside of her, and all she wanted for Christmas was more. Once their lips had touched, it had kindled the familiar yearning she had always carried for him. Any doubts she had about loving him evaporated like snow on a May day. She loved him with everything she possessed. Her heart, her happiness, her sorrow, and all her desires for life were his.

"Hello lass, I'm back." The deep reverberation of Cameron's voice pulled her from her musings, and she turned to greet him.

Resplendent in an iron gray dress coat and a green velvet waistcoat that magnified the color of his eyes and his chestnut hair, Cam was her very own Christmas present come calling.

She rushed to his side with her arms held out in greeting. "Cam, welcome." The breathlessness in her own voice couldn't be helped as she was delighted that he was here once again. Heat bludgeoned her cheeks from the intensity of his devouring gaze.

"Julia, you're more beautiful than the last time I saw you." He took her in his embrace, then gently kissed her cheek in welcome. When his cool cheek pressed against hers, it did little to bank the fire that had roared to life when she saw him.

"It's only been hours since we last saw each other." She took his hand and led him to the sitting area. "Come. Are you hungry?"

"Only for you," he whispered as he followed her.

Another blistering heat rolled through her. "Stop that or I'll not be able to serve you a proper tea."

A charming self-satisfied smile tugged at one corner of his mouth. "Hmm, I like the sound of 'not proper.'"

After they sat, Julia poured the tea and served Cam several pastries including a delicate mille-feuille filled with raspberry jam and several almond cakes sprinkled with crushed nuts. He accepted the plate without a word, then gently tugged her hand where a spot of jam stained her forefinger. Holding her gaze to his, he took her finger into his mouth and gently sucked.

She inhaled sharply as a bolt of electricity shot through her. The warmth of his mouth surrounding her skin melted her insides. But when his tongue moved against the sensitive skin, her gaze latched on his perfect lips and the slight indentation of his cheeks.

If she thought she'd experienced heat from his teasing, the sensations he summoned forth now could only be described as an inferno. Her heart pounded while her breath grew shallow. The force of their desire for one another caused a deep throbbing low in her middle. She closed her eyes so that all her concentration was focused on his mouth sucking her finger. Instantly, wicked thoughts of his mouth all over body threatened to consume her.

"Cam...I...we..."

He slowly withdrew her finger from his mouth but pressed it against his lips. "Hmm, I like that last bit, 'we.' Such a clever lass. I don't think I'll let you go."

The vibrations of his words against her wet skin caused her to shiver, but then his words registered. "What do you mean you won't let me go?"

"I want you all the days of my life and beyond, Miss Julia Lawson." He clasped her hand in his, then covered it with his other. "There is a solution to my dilemma, sweetheart."

The rumble of the endearment from his lips beguiled her, and she leaned forward. The smell of peppermint and male rose to greet her, and she breathed deeply.

"Marry me." He brought her hand to his lips. "Tell me you will, and I'll wait all day and all night outside McCalpin House, so I won't miss your sister and brother-in-law's arrival.

I'll fall to my knees in the snow and beg their permission." He pressed another kiss to the top of her hand. "I should have asked them before I spoke with you." He raked his free hand through his chestnut locks, the act causing a riot of curls to revolt by falling askew about his face. "But I love you, Julia. I don't want to lose you again."

The sincerity in his eyes caused her heart to pound against her ribs in a desperate act to reach him. "I love you," she said gently as tears flooded her eyes. "I always have and always will."

With the utmost care, he wiped one renegade tear that slid down her cheek, then pressed his lips against hers. With a sigh, she opened to him, and he deepened the kiss. His sweet taste and gentle lips told her how much he cared. In return, she kissed him with the same tender affection.

When he pulled away, he released an anguished breath, then pressed his forehead to hers. "I take that as a 'yes?'"

She could only nod.

He pulled her to him, and she pressed her ear against the middle of his chest. His heartbeat pounded like a coach and four barreling through the English countryside.

"Julia, let's not wait. I'll secure a special license. We can marry tomorrow morning, then head to Scotland directly after. If the fates and weather are kind, we can be nestled in bed together at Dunmore Castle within five days." He pulled away and cupped his cheeks in her hands. "We can be home. We'll spend our first Christmas and then every single one thereafter that the good Lord gives us in Edinburgh."

"Wait! No." She shook her head gently. "I can't leave Bennett."

His brow creased into neat lines.

She swallowed taking the moment to find the right words. "Bennett will feel abandoned, and I can't do that to him. You see, after we lost our parents and March and Faith married, he and I have become very close. He'd feel as if I've broken my vow to him. I just promised him this morning that I'd never leave him."

A beautiful smile lit his face. "There is no cause for concern. He'll come with us. Does he have a tutor or a governess? They'll come with us. If not, then we'll find the best tutor that Edinburgh has to offer. My nephews will need one, too. They can all study together."

The beguiling gleam in his startling gray eyes took her breath. Her beating heart pounded against her chest to reach his. She wanted to agree, but for all her worth, she simply couldn't. "Cameron, no. I can't take him from my sisters. The three of us are his security. He's learning how to be a man. Our brother-in-law, McCalpin, has personally taken him under his wing. He's teaching him what it means to be a peer and what those responsibilities entail."

Cam's eyebrow shot up, and his voice deepened. "I could teach him those skills, my love."

"Of course, you can. But it's more than that." If she navigated successfully through their conversation, perhaps they'd find a solution that would be satisfactory for them all. "Cam, you're an honorable and caring man. I wouldn't have fallen in love with you otherwise. It's just" —she twisted her fingers together— "that he's lost so much in his short life. I can't take him from his family."

He let out a soulful sigh. "Jules, if I was only responsible for myself, I'd say yes to staying in London. But I have my sister and my nephews to consider. I'm the only man in their lives now. I finally have Lara settled where she's able to grieve without the need to flee. I brought her and the boys with me so I could keep an eye on them. I can't ask her to stay in London. She might become distraught or fall ill again. If that happens, I'm not certain I can put the pieces together." He took her hands in his and gazed deeply into her eyes. "I can't jeopardize my family's safety and happiness. Perhaps in a year or so, we could spend more time in London. Until then, Bennett is always welcome in our home."

She blinked twice to defeat the sting of hot tears that threatened to escape. She had no conception that love could be so painful. Though she desperately wanted a life with him, her promise and duty were to her little brother. Just as Cam's duty required he care for his sister and nephews. Burrowed within her chest, her heart revolted by skipping a beat, but there remained only one right decision.

"I'm sorry, Cameron, but I can't marry you unless we stay in London and Bennett lives with us." She released his hands. The movement made her feel adrift in a sea of doubt as her heart and her mind battled against one another until there was only one clear victor who would take all the spoils of war, or perhaps more appropriately, the spoils of her heart. "Perhaps too much has transpired between the two of us in the six months that we've been separated."

He picked up the sprig of mistletoe that had fallen to the floor, then stood slowly. He studied the small posy as if it held answers to all their dilemmas. Finally, his sigh broke the silence between them. "I'm sorry too, Julia. I thought we'd be able to see our way through my mistakes...but perhaps I was foolish to hope for a Christmas miracle."

With a quick bow, he took his leave. The logs in the fireplace crackled before a flurry of sparks exploded.

Exactly what had happened to her heart when he exited the room. It shattered into a million pieces, and she had no idea how to put it together again.

Five

Julia sat in the salon not seeing or hearing anything until she found herself surrounded by her sisters, March and Faith. Her oldest sister March had brown hair that only enhanced her exquisite attractiveness. Julia favored her other sister in looks, but Faith's real beauty derived from her endless patience and kindness to all.

The concern on their faces opened the floodgates of grief and tears over losing Cameron. March rocked her in her arms as she'd done countless times when Julia was little and needed comfort. But there was no comfort and joy to be found this holiday.

After she had no more tears to expend, she released a deep breath. "It's over."

"What is?" Faith asked. She pushed a perfectly pressed linen square into Julia's hand.

"Queensgrace's and my betrothal. He asked me to marry him today, and I said yes. Then within a minute, it was over." The words sounded caustic to her ears, but she wanted to share her brief elation that had turned into such painful sorrow. If love could be so cruel, then she'd vowed she'd never subject herself to such agony again. But both March and Faith were the most level-headed women she knew. If anyone could help her heal, it would be them. Lucky for her they were her best friends as well as sisters. "He wanted to marry quickly, then move to Edinburgh as soon as possible." She forced herself not to succumbed to another sob that threatened.

"Why?" March asked as she brushed the wisps of Julia's hair that had escaped from the simple chignon she'd crafted this morning. "When you told us that he was coming today, we were thrilled that things seemed to be working out for the two of you. Don't you want to marry him?"

Julia shuddered in her arms, then pulled away. "More than anything. He explained why he hadn't written to me with more information. His sister was ill." That's all she felt comfortable sharing of the Queengrace family's misfortunes. "It's all I've ever wanted, but I made a promise to Bennett that I'd not leave him. Nor would I take him away from you both."

"Our brother is keeping you from marrying Queensgrace?" Faith tilted her head and studied her. "Julia, the earl loves you."

"I doubted him after he left me, but I have no doubt he loves me now," she murmured. "Sometimes love isn't enough. There are too many obstacles." Julia rose from her seat and began to pace. "Once Bennett discovered Cameron was in town, he's become very protective of me."

"That sounds like our brother," Faith agreed.

March's eyebrows lifted. "He's always done that. Is there more?"

She nodded. "He shared that he was frightened that I'd leave him. He believes we're the last of the Lawson family, and if I married and left to live with Queensgrace, then he'd be alone."

March sighed woefully, and little lines of worry creased Faith eyes.

"I've neglected him," March declared. Elegantly tall, she rose from her seat and joined Julia beside the fireplace.

"No, March. After all you've done to hold our family together, it was time for you to find happiness with McCalpin. I've never seen you so happy," Julia wouldn't let their oldest sister bear this burden—not after everything she'd done for the family. For years, she'd been the father, mother, estate manager, and governess to her brother and sisters.

Faith released a deep breath, then joined her sisters before the warmth of the fire. "Since I married Mark, I've been helping him as the demand for his services as a physician is increasing weekly. Perhaps, we could find someone else to help."

"No." Julia grasped her middle sister's hand in hers. "When you're with your husband, you absolutely glow with brilliance. You deserve such joy and more."

Julia bit her lip as the memory of Cam's mouth against hers cascaded through her thoughts. All afternoon she'd replayed their kiss. She promised herself she would never forget the soft sweep of his lips against hers or the way he deepened their kiss with his tongue as it tangled with hers. Now she knew how perfect such a heartfelt caress could be. No wonder poets were so effusive in their praise of the act. To forego Cam's kisses forever was her definition of purgatory, but her first responsibility was to Bennett.

"Perhaps we should call a family meeting," March offered. "Bennett's never been shy about telling any of us what he wants or needs. With the four of us, perhaps we can come up with a solution that will benefit us all?"

Faith nodded. "Just like in the old days."

Julia smiled at the fond memories. Though they were once a ragtag family, they always had loved each other deeply, and even when their circumstances had changed from dire to everything spectacular, they were loyal to one another. That's why she couldn't forsake her little brother.

She smoothed her hands over her shirt. "A family meeting won't change my mind. I'll not leave Bennett. All my life you two have provided the security for our family. It's my turn. It's a promise I intend to keep."

March stared at her. "Julia, even if it means you'll lose the love of your life?"

Gathering certainty in her decision, Julia attended to the fire, then turned to face her sisters. "How could I leave our brother after I promised him I wouldn't? I above all understand that feeling of abandonment."

The pain on March's face didn't escape Julia.

"March, you were everything to me when I was Bennett's age. I hate to think how I would have survived the loss of our parents without knowing that you were there for me. Always." She straightened her shoulders in a sign of strength. "You both have your husbands and other responsibilities that you're responsible for now just as I have mine. I want to be there for Bennett. Even though he acts like a man, he's still a little boy that deserves comfort, love, and a sense of belonging. I can provide that stability if I'm here in London. I can't do that in Edinburgh. Cam even offered to have Bennett live with us, but I'll not take him away from both of you."

Their eyes widened in shock. Even the suggestion of taking their little brother from them was inconceivable.

"Even if it means you're the one that sacrifices your happiness?" Faith asked softly.

"Yes. Christmas is the season where we should think of others first," Julia answered. Her chest tightened.

Even if marrying Cam was the only thing she'd ever wanted for Christmas.

Cam's London townhouse had always been a comfortable haven since he'd had it redecorated the first year he took his seat in the House of Lords. But the contentment he normally found within its walls had vanished. Even the Scottish tea he enjoyed first thing in the morning tasted like yesterday's bathwater.

He let out a deep breath as he studied the blanket of snow that covered the London streets outside his window. Would he ever find joy in the simple things in life again?

The inevitable answer of 'no' echoed throughout his musings. It'd been less than twenty-four hours since Julia had rejected his proposal. In that time, he hadn't come up with any additional arguments, let alone a sound solution to their problem. She needed London for her family, and he needed Scotland for his. Her sense of family and loyalty were some of her most endearing qualities. She'd shown that trait in abundance when they'd first met, and he'd been immediately smitten. That's why he could share so much and wanted to build a life with her.

He rested his head against the back of his chair and closed his eyes. He could propose that they marry, and she could stay in London when he had to travel to Scotland, but that left a bitter taste in his mouth.

He'd not leave his wife—his Julia again—ever.

But the truth was, she wasn't his.

"Cameron Alan Dunmore." Lara glided into the study. With her red hair and flashing blue eyes, she was a force to be reckoned with. "What have you done?"

Cam stood and studied her face. "Is something wrong?"

"Yes, something's wrong. I'm aghast. Are you really

thinking of leaving London without your bride?" Lara softened her voice. "You love her, Cam."

He came around the desk and led her to the two matching chairs in front of the fire. After she was seated, he took the other. "Too much has passed between Julia and me."

Her brow creased. "Is it because of me and my illness that you can't see your way clear to marry Julia?"

He took his younger sister's hand and squeezed. "No. She won't move to Scotland, lass, and I won't leave you and the boys."

She took a deep breath and sighed. "You were always the protector, Cam." She leaned close to him and held his gaze. "But let me take that role now. I thank you for everything you've done for me and mine, but it's time to live your own life. I'm better now. I'd even say I'm stronger now than ever before."

He had to make the right decision. Lara had only recently sewed the pieces of her life together with a proverbial thread that was still new and probably fragile. He couldn't live with himself if she fell ill again because of him. "There's no denying you're stronger," Cam said softly. "But I'd never leave you and the boys. You're my family."

"And so is Julia," Lara answered with a smile, but she held his gaze. "Listen to me, Cameron." She squeezed his hand in a show of strength. "I know what it's like to lose the love of your life. I'll not let you forgo such a gift as true love."

"My lord, a boy who calls himself Lord Lawson is here to see you." His butler and man-of-affairs, Dougan Campbell announced. "What shall I tell him?"

Lara stood and kissed his cheek. A breathtaking smile lit her face. Such a rare sight was a brilliant present in itself. "Find a way, Cam. It's what I want for Christmas," she said softly. "Now, see to your visitor."

"Send him in." Cam answered. As Lara left, he dropped

his shoulders. The young viscount probably still wanted to wring his neck for kissing his sister. Perhaps he should allow Bennett to do it. The pain wouldn't be any worse than the way his heart had been ripped in two after his last visit with his Julia. He closed his eyes. He was making himself sick with such thoughts. She wasn't his, and it appeared she never would be.

What a *bloody* happy Christmas this would be.

"Queensgrace?" Lawson entered the room.

Cam motioned him forward. The boy's normal bravado and keen sense of wicked humor were notably absent. Before Cam stood a tentative young boy, who seemed defeated.

"Lawson, I'm surprised you're here. What may I do for you this morning?"

"We need to talk man-to-man." Bennett's cheeks flushed, and he cleared his throat after his voice broke uncontrollably. A sign that the young boy in front of him would soon be on his way to manhood.

Cam blinked, then narrowed his eyes. The boy's face looked worried and a bit apprehensive. But Julia loved this boy with all her heart, and because she did, he'd welcome her brother into his home even though they both were aware that Bennett didn't trust him. "Come sit in front of my desk. Would you care for a tea or chocolate? The wind is particularly biting today."

The boy shook his head. "Thank you, but no. I'll be brief. Julia doesn't know that I'm here, and I'd like to keep it that way."

The boy's serious face gave Cam pause. "Would she disapprove?"

Lawson nodded gently. "After you left yesterday, Julia cried. I heard her tell my sisters that she couldn't marry you because of me."

The words were a direct punch in Cam's stomach, and he sucked a gulp of air. In all his years, he never recalled making a woman cry, and the fact that he'd made Julia, his love, cry left him reeling. "Lawson, I swear I never meant to hurt her."

With a slight nod that sent his black curls waving, the boy continued, "I'm aware that you love her, and this makes my confession doubly hard. I'm the one that made her cry. You see, I made her promise that she'd stay with me. But it was selfishness on my part. Julia, just like my other sisters, deserves happiness, and I know she'll have a happy life with you as your wife."

Cam leaned back in the massive study chair he'd had custom made to accommodate his long legs. The boy's solemn words were laced with contriteness. "That's very noble on your part, but I've never seen your sister as one who could be swayed if her mind and heart had decided another course." He leaned forward and rested his elbows on the desk as he regarded Bennett. "And if I could find a way around this predicament, trust me, I'd be on my knees in front of your sister right this minute begging her to marry me."

Bennett straightened in his seat and regarded Cam. "I've found a way. I've asked my tutor to recommend that I be admitted to Eton early for next term. March thought it best if I wait a year, so I had the necessary academic foundation, but I don't want Julia to suffer because I'm still at home. I'll see if there are private tutors that can help me acclimate to the academics required by the school."

Cam sat there dumbfounded. The boy sitting before him would make such a sacrifice for his own sister's happiness? "Bennett, you can come live with us in Scotland."

He shook his head. "I appreciate the offer, Queensgrace, but I need to think about what's right for my sisters. If I'm in school, then they can concentrate on their new families." The tiniest hint of an Adam's apple bobbed up and down on his thin neck. "They're all I have, and I'll see every one of them happy," he declared.

The unwavering strength in his voice that his decision was steadfast showed a maturity that grown men didn't possess. The Lawson sisters had raised a fine boy who would turn into a great man—sooner rather than later.

"It's my Christmas gift to all of them," he said. "Now, let me give you a piece of advice." He leaned close to Cam's desk, then lowered his voice. "Julia is shopping on Bond street for my present. Find her and walk with her a bit. She'll see how much she misses you. Tomorrow, McCalpin and March are having a Christmas Eve gathering for family and friends. I'm inviting you. You should ask her to marry you then." He winked, then delivered a sly smile. "No one can resist saying yes to a proposal on Christmas Eve."

Cam laughed at such an audacious comment coming from a ten-year-old boy. The charm he exuded would only increase the older and more confident he became. Ladies would soon be swooning at his feet. "And you know she'll say yes just because it's Christmas Eve, or is it because you have experience with the ladies?" He arched an eyebrow in obvious teasing.

"Well, McCalpin's cook is making me my very own Christmas pudding because she thinks I'm *enchanting*." Bennett waggled his eyebrows playfully. "But the answer to your question, Queensgrace, is no." He laughed in return. "Julia will say yes because she's madly in love with you."

Cam's heart swooped like a swallow returning home. Bennett truly knew the meaning of Christmas and the fact he was willing to sacrifice his own happiness for his sisters, particularly Julia, was awe-inspiring.

Having his heart desire's hand in marriage was everything Cam wanted this Christmas. Suddenly, a thought hatched that might make everyone's Christmas the best holiday ever.

"You're a man to be admired, Lord Lawson," Cam said. "You've given me some ideas. Where exactly did you say your sister is shopping?"

Six

Julia sensed Cam everywhere around her. From the scent of peppermint that reminded her of his kisses to the soft wool scarves that reminded her of his morning coat when his strong arms had held her. She could find a connection to Cam in every single item that surrounded her at Grigby's Haberdashery. With a deep sigh, she forced herself to admit it. After telling the earl she couldn't marry him, he haunted her day and night, particularly in her dreams when he'd take her in his arms and whisper sweet nothings while kissing her under boughs of mistletoe.

She shook her head slightly. She was a sorry example of a lovelorn goose. The quicker she finished her shopping, then the quicker she could prepare for tomorrow's small soiree at March and McCalpin's house. Most of McCalpin's family had traveled to Falmont, the Duke of Langham's ancestral home, for the holidays. But McCalpin and March, along with Faith and Mark, had friends who would visit tomorrow evening in celebration of Christmas.

Normally, she'd be overcome with excitement, but these

past several days had taken the joy out of the simplest things, including the holiday.

"Hello, Miss Lawson," a whisky dark voice murmured.

Without looking up, she'd recognize that deep cadence anywhere. It was *him*. Her heartbeat accelerated that Cam stood beside her. She forced herself to look up, and the sight stole her breath. He was magnificent in a subtle plaid morning coat with a deep red waistcoat and dark grey pantaloons. His Hoby boots glistened even though the London streets were somewhat mushy from the snow that had fallen two days ago.

"My lord," she answered. She straightened her shoulders and forced herself to smile. Though she couldn't marry him, at the very least, they should be friends, even if her contrary heart protested such an outcome. "It's good to see you."

"Is it?" he asked. A wry smile tugged at the corner of his lips.

She blushed at his obvious teasing. "You know that it is true. Every time..."

He leaned down and his grey eyes studied her. Her heart fluttered in her chest as if desperate to break free and reach him.

"Every time what, sweetheart?" His words floated over her, then he did the unthinkable. He caressed her cheek with the back of his finger, the touch soothing but at the same time making her want more, causing a heat that could never be satisfied.

"Whenever you're near, I'm happy. But you know that." Unable to control her joy at seeing him, a tremulous smile crossed her lips. "When are you going back to Scotland?"

"I'm not certain." A scowl marred his handsome face. "My plans have been upended."

"Because of me. I apologize that caused you such an inconvenience." She bit one lip, and his gaze narrowed to her mouth causing a heated blush to bludgeon her cheeks. "I wanted to say 'yes.' You believe me, don't you?"

She loved him so much that her heart ached. How could fate be so capricious and cruel at the same time, particularly at Christmas, when it brought him back into her life, but then not allow them to be together.

"Julia, I do. At first, I wasn't certain after we last parted. But just seeing your beautiful face light up"—his gaze caressed every inch of her face as if committing it to memory— "makes me believe you love me."

They would soon part for good, and she never wanted him to doubt her true feelings for him. In the past, when she'd thought these last six months were hard, she had no idea what would face her. The next six months without him promised to be unbearable. She could only survive it, and the years that would follow, if he realized that she would always love him. She didn't expect him to wait for her while Bennett grew to adulthood. But she also didn't want him to think that she'd rejected him because she didn't love him.

He caressed her cheek again. "You're so precious to me."

A hateful tear crept into her eye as his words surrounded her. How could she give him up? Then reason took over from her wayward emotions, and she remembered her commitment to Bennett. She put her gloved hand over his and squeezed. "I want you to promise me something." Before he could answer, she leaned close. "Never forget that I love you and always will. You'll never be alone. Miles may separate us, but you have my heart forever."

Without giving him a chance to respond, she quickly leaned up on tiptoes and gently pressed a kiss against his mouth. No well-respected young woman did such an outlandish thing out in public, but she didn't care. Deep in her heart, the truth couldn't be denied. If she couldn't marry

KISSES BY CANDLELIGHT

Cam, then she'd never marry. There was only man who could ever possess her heart, and she couldn't have him.

Before she said anything foolish or changed her mind, she darted out of the shop clutching the presents she'd carefully selected for Bennett.

At this moment, if she never celebrated Christmas again, it would be too soon. For the holiday only meant one thing to her now.

The day she lost the love of her life forever.

The lass's behavior left Cam bemused and somewhat flummoxed. All he'd wanted to do was to inform her of his plans for how they could be together. He rubbed a hand down his weary face before he suddenly realized what had occurred. It was his very own Christmas miracle. Julia Lawson would love him, Cameron Dunmore, forever with every fiber of her being.

Just like he would for her.

Unable to control his glee, he laughed aloud. The shopkeepers, Mr. and Mrs. Grigby, looked up from their work and smiled at the sound.

He nodded his greeting to the middle-aged couple, then turned his attention to the shop window. His darling, the lovely woman who had captured his heart, beat a fast retreat down the London street as if the devil himself were ready to claim her. But Cam had no cause to worry as he'd already claimed that enviable spot.

Julia Lawson was his now and forever, and he knew exactly how to woo his Christmas bride.

She'd see exactly what a Scotsman does when he wants a woman to take notice.

Seven

A new snow fell outside bestowing a holiday sparkle to the grounds of McCalpin House, but Julia couldn't muster any excitement. Crisp smells of the evergreen garlands and greenery that decorated the house filled the air. Guests surrounded her, and the sounds of holiday cheer melted together into a soft cacophony of merriment.

Never had she felt so alone.

March and McCalpin ushered a beautiful woman and two young boys into the sitting room. The woman was tall with dark red hair, and the boys resembled her. They were probably the wife and sons of some distinguished member of the House of Commons who her sister and husband had invited. The look of joy and contentment on her face pierced Julia's heart. Would she ever experience such feelings again? Not likely as her heart felt as if it had broken into a million pieces.

McCalpin stole a quick kiss from March under one of the bountiful boughs of mistletoe that seemed to reside over every doorway of the house. Those two were so in love, and their every action and deed seemed to magnify that fact.

Julia turned back to her study of the snow wanting the

night to be over with. She was surrounded by Christmas cheer, holiday love, and she wanted no part of it. Tomorrow she'd go to church and pray that her heartache would lessen, but it was unlikely. Every breath and thought reminded her of Cam.

"Julia, may I introduce Mrs. Lara MacFarland?" Somehow March had sidled up beside her with the woman and her two boys. Bennett stood next to the boys with a beaming smile.

"How do—" Julia gasped in a very unladylike manner. "You're Cam's sister?"

The woman smiled. "Indeed, Miss Lawson. It's lovely to meet you." She leaned close as if divulging a secret. "I've wanted to see for myself the woman who had enchanted my brother all this time." Her warm blue eyes twinkled in high spirits. "I can see why." She turned her gaze to the two boys beside her. "May I introduce my sons, Ewan, age eight, and Cameron, age six."

Julia smiled. They'd been named after Lara's husband and brother. "Hello. I'm—"

"She's my sister," Bennett announced, then turned to the guests. "Follow me. I know where the mince pies are. They're the best in London."

The boys' eyes widened in awe at Bennett.

"Do you know how to play chess?" Bennett asked.

"Uncle Cam is teaching us," Ewan answered.

Cam MacFarland nodded. "But I don't understand it yet."

Bennett waved his hand beckoning the boys to follow. "Come on then. Let's pile a plate full of sweets, then adjourn to the library. My old chess set is there. It's missing several pieces, but we can still play." Bennett put his arm around the littlest MacFarland lad. "Don't worry, I'll help you." He led the boys away all the while chatting about his prowess as a chess master.

Lara's smile made her radiant as she watched her sons retreat with Julia's little brother. "Lord Lawson has captivated my sons. I think they both have a serious case of hero-worship."

Julia smiled in answer. It was the first hint of lightness she'd felt all evening. "Thank you. My sisters and I adore him. I'm afraid we've probably spoiled him."

Lara leaned close. "That's what we're supposed to do with the irresistible men in our lives. Of course, that's my opinion, but wouldn't you agree?"

Julia grinned. "As long as they spoil us on occasion."

Lara laughed in answer. "I concur." Then her eyes grew misty. "I always spoiled my Ewan, and he did the same for me."

Julia grabbed her hand and squeezed. "Queensgrace told me about your loss. I'm so sorry."

Lara blinked rapidly, then squeezed in return. "I was fortunate that I had so many lovely years with him. After my husband died, I was so lost and ready to give up everything, but my brother made me realize that those two little men needed me to spoil them, too." She glanced around the room and took a deep breath. "May I call you Julia?"

"Of course," she replied.

"Julia, the one thing I've learned in this life is that when love is yours, you must hold on to it for as long as you have and cherish it." Her eyes glistened with emotion. "I lost my true love, but I never had any regrets. My husband and his love were the most precious gifts I'd ever received."

Before Julia could respond, a murmur went through the room, then complete silence. She looked up and immediately brought a hand to her mouth. Somehow, while she was talking with Lara, the entire room behind her had become flooded with vases of various shapes and sizes. Big bouquets of red roses crowded with boughs of mistletoe decorated the floor, the tables, even the fireplace. In the midst of all the green and red, Cameron stood in the doorway in full Scottish dress.

With snow covering his long hair, he looked like an ancient warrior prepared to win at any cost.

Instantly, her heart skipped a beat at the magnificent sight. But he stole her breath when his gaze captured hers. With heat and fire in his eyes, he came toward her without glancing at anyone else. Everyone stood off to the side to allow him a clear path.

In an instant, he stood before her. With his navy velvet evening coat, red and blue kilt, and matching waistcoat, he towered over everyone. The adornments on his sporran and the silver hilt of sgian-dubh glittered in the candlelight. Her breath caught at such a magnificent sight, and all she could do was stare.

"Julia, my love," he said tenderly. "Your brother and my sister helped me come up with a solution to our dilemma."

"What? When did they do that?" she asked incredulously as her breath grew shallow.

"Bennett came to see me yesterday right after Lara did." Cam took her hand in his and raised it to his lips. "Your brother loves you dearly. He offered to go to Eton early so we could marry."

Tears came to her eyes at her darling brother's action. Just then, she caught Bennett's gaze when he entered the room with Cam's nephews. He slightly bowed his head in acknowledgment.

"But I couldn't let the lad make such a sacrifice. Not when it came to his lovely sister. But with his and Lara's help, I thought of another solution."

Her heart was thudding against her ribs. Was it possible that she'd have her Christmas wish and be able to marry the man she'd fallen in love with? Tear streamed down her face, and Cam gently wiped them away.

"Don't cry, love. I promise you'll be happy if you still want me." The tenderness in his words flooded her with emotion.

"I'll always want you." She took the lapels of his jacket in her hands and gently pulled him closer. "Don't you know that? I love you with all my heart."

"And I love you with everything I am and everything I have to offer." He brushed his lips against hers, then pulled away.

The sound of happy sighs and gentle laughter filled the room, but she concentrated on the man she loved with every ounce of her being who stood before her offering the world.

Suddenly, he dropped to one knee while holding her hands. His strength and vibrance apparent in the heat of his large hands. "I've spoken with Lara and her sons. I told them I couldn't lose you, and like Bennett, they helped me find a way."

She couldn't answer as her throat tightened. Tears streamed down her face.

"They want to move to London. Lara wants a fresh start for herself and the boys here. Edinburgh holds too many painful memories for her. I don't have to return."

One of her hands flew to her mouth at his words.

"Now, I can do this properly and with the blessings of your family."

Julia's gaze darted to where Bennett, March and McCalpin, Faith and Mark stood. March and Faith's eyes glistened with emotion. McCalpin and Mark wore endearing smiles, but Bennett's smile took her breath away. He was beaming.

"Cam," she whispered.

He brushed another wayward tear from her cheek.

"Miss Julia Lawson, will you do me the greatest honor I could ever receive and be my wife?" The richness of his deep voice held a tenderness she'd never heard before. It filled the room with love and affection. "I bequeath my heart, my love, and everything I am to you. I promise to love you more each day and ensure your happiness to my utmost best. Please, give me your heart and hand in return."

"Forever," she whispered while she nodded for the crowd.

As applause and cries of good spirits rang out, Cam gracefully came to his feet and took her into his embrace. It felt like home, and Julia lifted her lips to his.

When his lips met hers, he tenderly kissed her. But as they stood in each other's arms, their passion swirled around them, binding them together in love while encompassing them in a cherished desire that would last forever.

Gently, Cam pulled away and cupped her cheeks in his warm hands. "I've got a special license in my pocket. We can marry tomorrow and make Christmas our special day always."

"I'd like that," she said shyly. "I don't want to spend another night alone without you."

"Clever lass." A grin spread across his face that could only be described as pure sin. "I was thinking the same. Come. Let's go somewhere we can have a little privacy."

Cam led her through the French doors to a balcony overlooking the main courtyard of McCalpin House. As he wrapped her in his arms, she forgot the cold and everything else except the man holding her tenderly.

"I love you, Cameron Dunmore. You've made me the happiest woman in London."

"I love you, Julia Lawson." He dipped his head to hers and gently rubbed his nose against hers. "You've made me the happiest man in Edinburgh. I've rented two townhouses next to each other. Lara and the boys will move into one, and we'll move into the other with Bennett." He pulled her tighter and pressed his lips to her temple. "We can move in immediately. Tomorrow if you like."

Julia tilted her head. "I hope I can wait that long."

Just then snowflakes danced through the air proving how magical the night had turned.

Cam chuckled as he looked up at the snow dancing in the sky. "Julia, look." He pointed above where a bouquet of mistletoe hung from the overhang above them.

"Did you put that there," she teased.

"And ordered the snow." Gently, he kissed the tender spot below her ear. "Anything for my Christmas bride."

He took her lips with his and kissed her with a tender passion that made her believe all her dreams had come true. She returned his kiss with an equal passion that told him she'd never let him ago. In that perfect moment, their lips met in a searing kiss that bespoke of Christmas, magic, and the promise that such miracles would always be a part of their lives —forever.

The End

Red Ribbons and Rogues

Red Ribbons and Rogues

Ordinarily, the smells of mulled wine and evergreens made Miss Eve Marchant happy—not just happy—but ecstatic for her favorite time of the year. The scents combined into an enchantment that surely brought forth all sorts of Christmas magic. She only hoped that miracles were a byproduct of some of that elusive magic.

She desperately needed one tonight.

Cocooned in the library with a beloved book, she gritted her teeth. She'd tried five times to read the same page, but merrymaking sounds from the crowded salon down the hall interrupted her peace. Earlier, she'd entered the room where festive couples danced, flirted, and when they thought no one was looking, stole kisses from each other. Ostentatious displays of mistletoe decorated with bright ribbon and ivy hung from every available doorway, window latch, and staircase landing.

All this revelry was enough to convince Eve that a Christmas faery had landed in their midst and had cast a spell over everyone except her. Taking a sip of her family's famous —not to mention—delicious, mulled wine, Eve peeked at the library door wishing for a little holiday miracle to come her way—her very own Christmas beau to walk right into the room.

A year ago, she'd thought it inevitable that she'd have such a man.

Someone who would take her skating at the pond at twilight.

Someone who would keep a handy sprig of mistletoe in his pocket for yuletide kisses under the staircase.

Someone who would seek her hand in marriage.

That someone, namely Julian deLisle, the Earl of Winterford, hadn't spared a glance Eve's way when he'd entered her home this evening for the holidays. Accompanied by a beautiful woman who reminded Eve of a regal ice queen, Julian had immediately swept the woman into his arms right under the mistletoe that guarded the entry door.

Eve had waited all day for his arrival. At the sight of Julian and the woman in an embrace, anger, hotter than a blacksmith's fire, had blasted through her. She'd vowed not to subject herself to the torture of watching Julian kiss another woman. The only safe course was to find a refuge. Some place she could collect her composure.

The library, her favorite place in the house, always had provided succor when she needed it. She and Julian had shared their first kiss in this very room last Christmas. Eve had thought this holiday...well, what she thought was foolish if she believed Julian would declare his intentions this Christmas.

The smell of the library's evergreen boughs did little to calm Eve's ire. Her mind refused to quiet. Right now, the cad was probably holding court under the mistletoe with every available female attending the family's annual Christmas Eve party.

A dull ache throbbed in her chest. She'd tried to blame her suffering on the extra serving of fruitcake she'd had after dinner, but deep down she couldn't deny the truth. It was Julian.

Eve straightened her shoulders and forced her attention back to her book. Always a tad willful, she decided to push her unhappiness aside like long-forgotten toys of Christmas past.

She'd not let that bounder's behavior have any further effect on her.

The library door swept open, and the happy sounds from the party rushed in like meddlesome busybodies. Without looking up from her book, she let out an exasperated sigh.

"The room is occupied."

Surely, the intruder would *see* and *hear* they were not welcome.

"Could you squeeze in another?" a man whispered.

Eve's feigned attention to her book snapped at Julian's husky-dark voice.

The wretched rogue took command of the room like a formally dressed pirate—tall, dark, and dangerously handsome. Her perfidious eyes traveled the length of his body from his perfectly shined boots to his immaculate evening coat. The elegant tailoring of his clothes emphasized his perfect physique. His black hair glistened in the candlelight making her fingers itch to tangle in the long locks.

She made the mistake of glancing at Julian's face. His enchanting blue eyes twinkled with delight. Her bravado immediately deflated as her resolve melted.

"Go away, Julian," she whispered. "I want to be alone."

Her mind screamed "liar," as she pursed her lips to keep from asking him to join her.

"I can't. I have an assignation planned this evening." A wicked smile tugged at his lips. "In this very room."

She could only stare at his boldness. In this very room, they'd shared kisses last Christmas, but the kiss they'd shared during the late autumn was tantamount to a proposal. Had she mistaken his affections? With an unladylike gasp, she drew a deep breath. It would be her luck that Julian—of all the people in the kingdom—would pick her hideaway to meet a woman.

"When?" Eve asked. What she really wanted to know was with whom, but she'd not lose her dignity by asking.

"Shortly. However, I'm glad you're here. I have something for you." He pulled a small package wrapped in plain paper and tied with a red ribbon. "This evening, I've given a token of the season to all the ladies present. I kept yours for last."

With as much grace as she could muster, Eve stood. "What is it?"

Julian closed the distance between them, then handed her the gift. "Open it, and find out."

She untied the ribbon and slipped the paper free. Inside was a small book hardly bigger than the palm of her hand. When she opened the first page, there was a small painting of a blazing yule log in a fireplace. The image so lifelike, she could almost feel the heat radiating from the fire.

She peered up at his face and wished she hadn't. His eyes flashed with excitement, another reminder of how devastatingly handsome he was. "It's beautiful. Did you paint it yourself?"

He nodded. "Turn the page."

A vase with an arrangement of red roses, holly, and ivy was the subject of the second painting. Her favorite flower and greeneries combined. "Oh, Julian," she whispered. "You're very talented."

The words were sorely inadequate to describe his work. Each piece of art displayed his amazing ability to capture something so ordinary in life and turn it into something breathtaking. Unsurprisingly, each page revealed his wonderful passion for life. A passion she wanted to share. An unwanted rush of tears blurred her eyesight. She willed them away with a blink. "I don't have a gift for you."

"Maybe you'll have one for me later," Julian whispered as he smiled again. "Go to the next one."

The next few pages depicted a sleigh with horses bedecked in bright festive ribbons and bells, followed by a gathering of carolers outside on a snowy night. The next was a cornucopia of holiday delights—a plum pudding, mincemeat pies, and roasted chestnuts. Page after page contained miniature paintings and sketches of her favorite things at Christmastide—snow on a moonlit night, perfect icicles lined in a neat row, a church sanctuary decorated throughout with evergreens, two pairs of skates hanging from a barn hook, and a tabletop teeming with the recipe ingredients for her family's mulled wine and two mugs.

"These are my favorite things at Christmas." Carefully, she trailed her fingers around the corners of the book. "This must have taken you months to paint and draw. Did you do this for every woman here?" she asked incredulously.

"Your book took me about six months to create. Go to the last page, and I think you'll have the answer to your question."

Eve nodded without looking at him. If he smiled again, she'd make a fool of herself with her wayward tears. She had to remember he had "an assignation" later on in this very room. She knew she shouldn't, but her curiosity always got the better of her. Before she turned the page, she had to know whom he was meeting—even if it broke her heart.

"Are you meeting the woman you brought to the party?" Her voice trembled, betraying her misery. With tears in her eyes, Eve stared at the book fearful to look anywhere else. It was stupid to have spoken the words aloud, and secretly, she hoped for both their sakes he didn't answer.

"Is that why you're angry with me?" Gently, he tugged her chin upward. "Look at me, Eve."

She blinked once for fortitude, then forced her gaze to his.

"The woman I brought to the party is my widowed cousin, Isabelle. She's alone this Christmas. I asked your brother if I could bring her. I wanted to come to you sooner, but I needed to introduce Isabelle to everyone before I came to see you. No, I'm not meeting her here."

One renegade tear fell. "I'm so foolish."

"No. You aren't." Gently, he pressed his lips against hers, then drew back. "You are a brilliant and beautiful woman. Now, turn the page."

With trembling fingers, she managed to flip to the last page. There was no sketching, but two words, *Marry me?*

Her gaze flew to his. The uncertainty in his eyes was something she'd never seen.

"That's the gift I want for Christmas. Will you marry me?"

For a moment, his words robbed her ability to speak. Julian was proof that Christmas miracles were real.

"Yes, I'll marry you." Her tears, laughter, and utter joy combined into a maelstrom she couldn't control, and she didn't care. Without hesitating, she launched herself into his arms. "I love you."

Julian kissed her with a tender passion that made her knees weak. He held her tight as if he'd never let her go.

She definitely would never let him go.

"Now, you know the identity of the woman I was meeting here for my assignation." Gently, he kissed the tender spot right below her ear. "The love of my life."

Never Enough Mistletoe Kisses

A SHORT STORY

Never Enough Mistletoe Kisses

Miss Clarissa Bickham bit her lip to keep from cursing her older brother, John Bickham and his new wife, Jane. Their grandfather, Mr. Nelson Bickham, had sent Clarissa to collect another cup of mulled wine, but the newlyweds blocked the refreshments from all sides. Then John had the audacity to pull out his mistletoe sprig and leaned close to Jane for a kiss. After what had to be a least a minute, John finally pulled away, then plucked one berry from the bundle. Immediately, he eyed his wife as if wanting another. Without further ado, he kissed his wife soundly. Jane grinned and a delightful smile lit John's face.

If they did it one more time, Clarissa would have no recourse but to dump her grandfather's mulled wine over their heads. It wouldn't be her fault if the happy couple were outraged. It'd been her grandfather's idea to give every man and woman over the age of sixteen a sprig of mistletoe with berries as a welcoming gift for attending the annual holiday house party at Bickham Manor. Even her parents, Mr. and Mrs. Charles Bickham had been delighted with their sprigs.

Frankly, it was a little nauseating. Clarissa had never seen such a vast amount of kissing and laughter and silliness over a parasitic plant. However, she had no one to blame except her grandfather's sudden change of heart.

Truthfully, there was only one way to describe her grandfather.

A curmudgeon.

He normally desisted having everyone descended upon Bickham Manor during the holiday season and let everyone know about his displeasure by growling and snarling throughout the festivities. Their grandmother always ignored his antics, but his predictable behavior was the reason her brother John called him Badger behind his back instead of grandfather.

But for some odd reason, this holiday season their grandfather had softened his attitude during Christmastide. He even smiled and laughed at all the frivolity and the accompanying glee that surrounded him this year.

But this flurry of romantic behavior by the rest of her family bordered on excessive.

"Come, girl. Where's my wine?" Her grandfather bellowed.

"I'll be there shortly, but John and Jane are—"

"Kissing again?" Her grandfather giggled like a schoolboy. "Do they have any berries left?"

"We're down to our last two," John answered while Jane's cheeks flushed a brilliant red.

"Two, too many," Clarissa mumbled.

"What's that, girl?" Her grandfather motioned her to his side.

Jane handed her a new cup of mulled wine. "I apologize for keeping your grandfather waiting."

Clarissa nodded her head in thanks.

"Do try to smile, Clarissa," John chided. "You're so much prettier when your lips are turning up instead of down."

She ignored her older brother's teasing and went to stand by her grandfather's side.

He took a sip of the wine and sighed in relief. "I don't know why we don't have this all year round. Seems a shame to only serve once a year."

For the first time that evening, Clarissa smiled. It wasn't even one of her usual forced smiles, but an affectionate one.

"There's my girl's smile. I've missed it." Her grandfather patted her hand, his touch warm and comforting. "Christmas is for smiles and celebrations."

Her breath hitched at his softly spoken words. "Not hearing from Ethan for six months takes the joy out of the season for me."

Her grandfather nodded. "I don't know what I'd do if I didn't hear from your grandmother for six months."

"Not seeing or hearing from my beloved is like having a hole where my heart should reside." She reached inside her dress pocket and fingered her sprig of mistletoe her grandfather had given her. Since she'd arrived at Coventry Crossing, her grandparents' home, Clarissa went to bed every night dreaming she'd kissed Ethan. In his honor, she always picked a berry in the morning. Now there was only one left on her mistletoe.

She closed her eyes and shook her head sharply. She should throw the *bloody* thing out. It was a hurtful reminder of all she'd lost this year.

"You think he's never coming home?" her grandfather asked gently.

A sharp pain in the center of chest caused her breath to catch. Though he didn't mean to, his simple question gutted her. She took a deep breath and swallowed the pain the best she could. "I can only hope he'll come home one day."

Tonight, she and Ethan Thornton, the second son of the Earl of Hawkridge, had planned to marry at Coventry

Crossing during the annual party. But last spring, Ethan had been sent on a secret mission to France behind enemy lines. His last missive to her was six months ago. She hadn't heard from him since.

"I'm sorry, my girl." Her grandfather bowed his head for a moment as if saying a prayer, then lifted his gaze to hers. "But you need to keep the faith. Hope only goes so far."

Clarissa's grandmother, Elizabeth Bickham, sidled up beside them. "You two are gloomier than January in London. We can either bring in more mistletoe and holly or open presents this Christmas Eve."

"Mistletoe." Her grandfather scrunched his nose. "It's more fun."

Clarissa took her grandfather's advice then and there and said a little prayer. *Dear God, please let grandmother convince him to open presents. I can't bear to see another happy couple kiss. Not now, not tonight.*

Her grandmother pulled her sprig of mistletoe, then examined it. "I have two berries left. Who do you think I should share them with?"

Her grandfather's hand shot out, and he pulled his wife onto his lap, the quick movement belying his age. "Those berries are mine."

"Just like you're mine," her grandmother whispered.

Her grandfather chortled. "Always and forever, my dear wife." He turned to Clarissa as he tucked her grandmother closer to his chest. "My girl, why don't you go to the small study and give your grandmother and me some privacy. Your present is there." Without waiting for an answer, he turned back to his wife and kissed her soundly on the lips.

Clarissa practically ran down the hall to escape the happy noise and the loving sight of seeing her grandparents together. Scalding tears pooled in her eyes. She was delighted that they had such a loving marriage, but tonight, all she wanted was to see Ethan one more time.

Quickly, she arrived at study door and twisted the knob. She stepped into the cozy room where a large fire held court behind her grandfather's familiar desk. Some of her fondest memories were in this room. She closed her eyes as the memories rushed forward to greet her. It was where she first met Ethan. They'd even shared their first kiss together here last Christmas, then made plans for a life together.

She willed herself to stop such thoughts as a rogue tear escaped. She'd best find the present, open it here in private, then thank her grandparents before making the excuse of a megrim so she could go to her chamber and grieve. She pushed away from the door determined to find her present and end her torture.

That's when she noticed him gazing out the bay window into an endless black night. Even without the light reflected by the fire, she would have recognized him immediately.

"Ethan, you've come home." Her voice trembled. "Thank God in heaven, you're home." She rushed forward to embrace him but stopped when a mere foot separated them. He still hadn't turned around. Gently, she reached out and touched his shoulder. "Ethan, it's me, Clarissa."

Still facing the window, he bent his head as if deciding what to do. He'd always been tall, but in the last year, he'd become broader in the shoulders, and more muscular all over. She always thought him handsome, but tonight with his blond hair brushing his shoulders, he reminded her of an angel, perhaps an archangel.

"Clarissa." The familiar husky whisper sent delicious chills through her. Without another word, he pivoted on one heel and faced her.

A patch covered his left eye.

She subdued her shock at his haggard appearance and looked her fill as her gaze caressed his. He looked tired and weary from his travels, but he was alive and had come back to her. She didn't ask what had happened as she already knew. He must have been injured while working for their king and country.

For one long moment, they stared at each other. Unable to bear being separated any longer, she launched herself into his arms. "My love, you're finally here."

Her sudden movement took him by surprise, and he stumbled backwards before righting himself. His arms tightened around her, and in his embrace, she felt like she was finally home.

"Ethan." His name escaped like a solemn vow. "I love you. How I've missed you." Happy tears streamed down her face. "Every day I wondered where you were."

He drew back, and his deep green eye narrowed. "You have no idea how I've missed you." He raised a hand and caressed her cheek. "This is what I dreamed of every night—what kept me alive. You, standing before me. You brought me home. I refused to die over there without seeing you again."

She leaned forward hungry for his touch and for him. When he didn't lower his head for a kiss, she clasped her hands around his neck and lifted herself on tiptoe. "Kiss me."

He stiffened and closed his one eye. "Does it...bother you?" He didn't move as he waited for her to speak.

There was only one way to answer.

She pressed her lips against his. Everything that was wrong with her world righted itself in that instant. She deepened the kiss, and he let her. As her tongue met his, she shared all her joy, hopes and dreams in that tender kiss. She wanted him as he was. Though she was angered and saddened that he suffered, it didn't keep her for wanting to rejoice that their own Christmas miracle had happened.

Eventually, she drew away desperate for another look at his face. "Does that answer your question?"

He nodded gently, then rested his forehead against hers. More intimate than a kiss, he gently rubbed his nose against hers. "You'll still marry me?"

"My lovely, foolish, dear man. Didn't my kiss answer your question." She reached up and pressed her lips to his then whispered. "Yes, I want to marry you. More today than yesterday, and more tomorrow than today. I'll kiss you all night just to convince you."

He laughed, and the merry sound was more welcome than church bells on Christmas morning.

"How long were you waiting for me? Why didn't my grandfather and grandmother tell me straight away?" Needing to touch him, she combed her fingers through his soft hair.

Ethan traced a finger across her lips. "My darling"—his deep voice rumbled with emotion—"I asked your grandfather not to send you straight away." He exhaled. "I had to gather my courage to face you."

Her heart pounded as she realized how difficult it had been for him to come to her. "Thank you."

"For what?" His gaze searched hers.

"For finding the strength to come home to me. For loving me." She kissed him again. For as long as she lived, she'd never have enough of his kisses. She now understood her grandfather's wishes for the mistletoe sprigs this year. She pulled her sprig out of her pocket with the single berry left.

"What do you have?" Gently he took the tiny sprig. His large hands and long fingers dwarfed the greenery.

"Grandfather gave everyone a sprig this year so they could have kisses whenever they wanted. He said kisses were to be cherished and enjoyed anytime and anywhere."

"Wise man," Ethan said with a chuckle. "You only have one berry left?"

She looked into his gaze, and all she could see was their happy future. She smiled, and he smiled in return.

"Every night, I kissed you in my dreams. Each morning, I picked a berry in honor of our kisses. This is the only one I have left."

"Then we'd best make the most of that single berry." He leaned close and touched his lips to her ear. "Look behind you."

She turned to discover the largest branch of mistletoe she'd ever seen under a table. "There must be hundreds of berries on that branch.

"Your grandfather told me he saved the biggest branch for my sprig." Ethan's familiar, deep rumble of laughter tickled her ear. "I think we're going to be busy for a while."

Her kissed her again with such fervor that Clarissa had little doubt that all of her Christmas wishes had come true.

"Your grandfather is a wise man."

"I agree. One can never have enough mistletoe kisses."

Happy holidays!

Kissing Boughs and Pampered Pugs

A SHORT STORY

Kissing Boughs and Pampered Pugs

"Poppy, you are a harlot," Jane Hosmer said laughing.

Her pet pug lay on her back in the middle of the bed with all four paws in the air. The pose, a favorite of the precocious canine, was designed to elicit a much-needed chest rub.

"You poor darling," Jane cooed as she stroked the fawn fur of Poppy's chest. Her fingers sank into the softness and a snort of approval erupted from Poppy. "You know all the right things to say to entice me to continue."

Poppy's big brown eyes looked adoringly at Jane. She had the same look for her real owner, Heath Lovelady, when she'd last seen him three years ago. That was before he went to Brussels on a special assignment for Wellington, and he'd asked Jane to take care of his dog. Of course, Jane had said yes. Heath was Jane's brother's best friend. He was also the man Jane had given her heart to when she was ten years old. At the age of twenty-two, she still didn't have it back.

Wherever Heath was, that's where her heart resided.

Jane glanced out the window where the snow swirled in a familiar winter dance. Inside, a beautiful fire blazed in the bedroom's fireplace and a lovely glass of mulled wine waited for her on the table beside her.

She picked it up and toasted the snowfall. This made the third Christmas that she'd be without Heath. She took a sip wondering whether she ever crept into his thoughts like he did hers. Jane cast such thoughts aside. It was Christmas and she would not allow herself to be sad. It was a time of family and new beginnings.

None of the other guests had arrived at her aunt and uncle's home for their annual holiday house party. They might not arrive until late tomorrow if the snow continued falling. Within the hour, the landscape had turned into a frosty wonderland. It was beautiful but frigid outside. Frost was already forming on the inside of the windows.

"You're not going to make me take you out in this, are you, Poppy?"

The pug flipped on her stomach. With a loud canine sigh, she closed her eyes.

"Thank goodness," Jane whispered. She stood, then finished her ablutions. She threw on an old-discarded banyan that Heath had left at her house right before he traveled to Belgium. Though it was Jane's personal keepsake, the silk was so worn that Jane feared she might wear a hole in it. It wouldn't matter. It still carried Heath's scent. She inhaled deeply, then settled in front of the fireplace. As the fire warmed her outside, the wine warmed her on the inside. She let her thoughts wander to Christmas and couples. What must it be like to celebrate with a special someone such as a man who would only have eyes for you? The small desk clock chimed the midnight hour signaling she should go to bed. But it was Christmas time, and visions of Heath Lovelady danced in her head.

Scratch, scratch, scratch.

Jane's eyes flew open, and she looked toward the door.

Poppy stood next to it with a look that commanded Jane to attend her.

"Of all the nights," Jane murmured as she stood to put on her half-boots and take the dog outside. "Just a second, Poppy." She threw a dressing gown that tied at the waist over the bayan, then turned toward the door.

Just then, the pug pawed the door open a crack.

"Poppy, come here." Jane's call sounded woefully like she was pleading.

Without a glance back, Poppy shook herself, then pranced right out into the hallway without a look goodbye.

"Poppy, get back here," Jane cried as she followed the dog.

The pug slowed and took a gander at Jane. Without even a hint of remorse, she turned back around and increased her speed while continuing her path. Poppy was in rare form this evening. She was practically flouncing down the hallway. Suddenly, she stopped in front of a bedroom door where golden light spilled into the hallway. Another guest had arrived before the storm had hit.

"Poppy," Jane commanded. "Stop."

The pug turned its head and took a disinterested gander at Jane.

"Come, girl. I have a *treeeeat*." Jane coaxed. She actually didn't, but as soon as she had the dog in her arms, she'd find one.

But only on the condition the dog came to her. Immediately, for instance, like in the next seconds.

"You want a treat?"

Poppy cocked her head at the word 'treat.' Then, as all pugs are wont to do—ignore their masters—the dog curled her tail a little tighter in defiance, then marched straight into the bedroom.

"You just proved why I should have insisted that I was

allergic to you," Jane said to no one but herself. She crept slowly down the hall praying the bedroom was empty.

"Well, hello," a deep male voice drawled. It sounded like an invitation for pure sin, one that a woman could surrender everything to. "How fine you look this evening. Don't dawdle, my beauty. Let me hold you."

This was bad.

Poppy had found and was about to interrupt a liaison. Loving whispers escaped followed by a kissing noise.

This was very bad.

Jane closed her eyes desperate to think of something. What was the proper protocol for interrupting a lover's tryst? Almost afraid to breathe, she forced herself to peek around the corner.

Bother. Poppy was nowhere in sight. But a man, fit and trim, stood with his back to her. Without a waistcoat, his white linen shirt was stretched across his broad back.

Good heavens, he was lovely, and with a look down his trim and muscular form, Jane discovered *he was barefoot*. She decided then and there she would deny that pampered pug treats for a week over this. Jane didn't care if it was Christmas.

There was only one thing to do: Announce herself, knock on the door, breakup the interlude, then get her dog and apologize.

She took a deep breath for fortitude. It was now or never. "Excuse me," she said, knocking on the door gently. "I've lost my dog."

"Oh, you darling girl of mine, where have you been? I love your perfume." The man laughed, then made another smooching sound.

Obviously, she hadn't been loud enough. For the love of pugs, she had to get that *bloody* dog out of there. The thought occurred to her that perhaps Poppy deserved to be in the bedroom with the couple all night. That would teach her she should be loyal to the person who gave her belly rubs.

Jane stepped through the door. "I apologize for interrupting."

The man turned around in a slow elegant manner.

"My dog..."

In his arms, he held Poppy. Both looked guilty as if they'd been caught in the act. But Jane's ire immediately melted at the sight of one of Heath's lopsided grins. "You're home!"

"Janie! Is that really you?" Holding Poppy tucked under one arm, he rushed to her side and brought her close for a one-armed hug.

At the feel of his arm around her, she breathed deep. He still smelled the same, looked the same, and possessed the same sweet smile and twinkle in his eyes. He bent his head and kissed her...on the cheek.

Just like a sister.

A pang of disappointment deflated her newfound jubilance.

Of course, he would only see her as his best friend's little sister. She couldn't expect anything more. She should be delighted he was home, but she'd changed and hoped he saw it too. He'd certainly come home different. Wider, taller, more masculine—simply put, he was more handsome than a man had a right to be.

Jane fought to hide her disappointment at the friendly kiss. "You look well, Heath."

He blinked slowly, the movement emphasizing his long lashes. With his blond hair and blue eyes, he reminded her of a Christmas tart—sweet and succulent. She glanced at his feet again, and her cheeks heated betraying her thoughts.

"As do you, Janie," he murmured in a voice that was softer than black velvet. Then he smiled, and the entire room seemed to brighten. "We're the only ones here, I take it?"

"Robbie is with my parents. I think they must be caught in the storm."

Heath nodded, still stroking Poppy's fur.

For the moment, Jane found herself actually jealous of the pug, a dog she had doted on and loved for the last three years. She reached out and stroked the pug's head. Her fingers tangled with Heath's, and a spark of something arced between them.

Jane hissed softly and pulled her hand back. Her gaze collided with his.

He studied her as if trying to solve a puzzle. Then his eyes blazed brighter than a yule log. Unable to move, Jane was caught in his heat. He leaned close, and there was little doubt...he was going to kiss her.

This was everything she'd ever dreamed of. It would be the best Christmas ever.

"Thank you for taking such good care of her." He drew nearer. "I hope she wasn't too much trouble," he said softly.

"No." Jane tilted her mouth to his.

Then he dipped his head and pressed those full, perfect lips to the top of Poppy's head.

※

Bloody hell. He'd waited three years to kiss Janie, but instead, he'd kissed Poppy. This was the perfect opportunity, but his damned conscience interrupted the moment.

He exhaled. It was just as well. He'd not dishonor Janie by kissing her in his bedroom when she was in her bedclothes, and he was barefoot.

But soon he'd take her in his arms, then kiss her like he'd dreamed about for three years. He didn't care where they were or who saw them. Besides, it was Christmastide. If anyone deserved a treat for being good, it was Heath.

Jane was still as vibrant as she always had been. When she'd seen his bare feet, she'd blushed a brilliant red. It reminded him of a perfect crimson poppy, his favorite flower. Well, the night was still young, and he had a certain someone special he wanted to spend the evening with.

"What were you doing out in the hallway?" Heath asked, but he couldn't quit staring at Janie. When he'd first left for the war, she still had the appearance of a young woman about her, but now...she was a beauty...a full-grown woman who mesmerized him.

Jane smiled slightly. "I was going to take Poppy out until she wandered in here. I thought...you had a woman in here."

"Who would I have?" he asked incredulously. "No one except you, dear Janie."

She tugged the belt of her dressing gown a little tighter, but it gapped at the chest.

His eyes widened. "What are you wearing?"

She grasped the gown about her neck. "Just something old."

He laughed softly. He knew exactly what it was. "Is that my old bayan?"

She nodded. "I saved it." Her voice softened. "I thought if I took care of it for you, you'd come home and claim it."

He wanted to claim it that very instance with her inside of it. "Were you worried for me, Jane?" he murmured. Slowly, he reached out with his forefinger and rubbed her cheek. She leaned into his touch and closed her eyes.

"Yes," she said.

"I'll take the dog outside."

"I'll come with you," she answered, then added quickly. "And Poppy."

Heath took a deep breath and slowly released it. "Good. There's something I want to show you."

While Heath and the dog were outside, Jane marveled at the main floor. Since she'd arrived, the staff had completely decorated the rooms including the entry and hallway with bright, festive holly and other evergreens. It smelled of Christmas as the scent of delicious fruit breads and cake filled the air.

Thankfully, Poppy did her business quickly.

With a determined step and cheeks reddened by the cold, he walked toward her, the pug trailing behind.

Jane would remember this night for the rest of her life. Even if their futures were never tied together, they had *something* they shared together.

This special night of Christmas.

"What did you want to show me," she whispered.

"Look," Heath pointed above them.

A huge kissing bough decorated with mistletoe, holly, and roses hung directly above them.

Jane's heart started to accelerate, but she forced herself to lower her gaze to Heath.

His eyes smoldered, and he closed the distance between them. In a slow exaggerated movement, he took her arms. "Jane, I'm going to kiss you," he whispered.

"Please." Her voice sounded breathless to her own ears. This was heaven in his arms.

He lowered his lips to hers.

Jane sighed, and he deepened the kiss. He stroked his tongue against hers.

This was everything she'd dreamed of for Christmas.

Heath moaned as he brought her closer, and she answered in kind. Their kiss was a conversation where they shared all their gratitude and joy for this special night and each other.

Eventually, Heath pulled away, then cupped her cheeks as he pressed another kiss to her mouth. "Poppy and I had a long conversation."

That wasn't what Jane had expected him to say, but the wicked grin on his face convinced her to play along. "Indeed? I'm agog to hear what she has to say."

Heath trailed his lips up her neck until he nibbled on Jane's ear. "She says that she doesn't want to come home with me...unless you do."

Jane bent her head to allow him better access. "What does that mean?"

"Marry me, Janie." Heath gazed into her eyes. "Give me the one thing I want for Christmas. Make me the happiest man in all of England."

Jane stilled. "Really?"

"Truly," he answered.

Tears came to her eyes, but she couldn't stop smiling. "Yes. A hundred times, yes. It's all I wanted for Christmas."

Heath rested his forehead against hers. "It's all I wanted, too." He drew back and captured her gaze. "But there's several things we'll have to discuss. When shall we marry? Where? I want it to be as soon as possible."

Jane nodded her head in agreement. "But there's one question that has to be answered tonight." She reached up on her tiptoes and pressed a kiss to his lips. "Make that two questions. I love you. Do you love me?"

Heath leaned back and laughed. "I think I've loved you since you were ten. What's the second question?"

"Where shall Poppy sleep? With you or me?"

Heath pressed another kiss against his beloved's lips. Even

when they were ninety, he'd never tire of her and her sweet kisses. "Where do you think she'd want to sleep?"

"Poppy also shared something with me. She wants to sleep with both of us." Jane waggled her eyebrows.

"I always knew she was brilliant. Let's not keep the poor darling waiting, shall we?"

Jane released a contented sigh as she pressed another kiss to Heath's lips. "No, we should not. Christmas, snowstorms, kissing boughs, and pampered pugs should not be wasted."

Other Books by Janna MacGregor

If you enjoyed *The Earl's Christmas Bride* (The Cavensham Heiresses) by Janna MacGregor be sure to look for other titles in this series.

THE BAD LUCK BRIDE
THE BRIDE WHO GOT LUCKY
THE LUCK OF THE BRIDE
THE GOOD, THE BAD, AND THE DUKE
ROGUE MOST WANTED
WILD, WILD RAKE
Don't miss Janna's latest series, THE WIDOW RULES
WHERE THERE'S A WILL
A DUKE IN TIME
RULES FOR ENGAGING THE EARL
HOW TO BEST A MARQUESS
Keep reading for an exclusive peak...

To find out more about Janna or to sign up for her newsletter visit www.jannamacgregor.com.

OTHER BOOKS BY JANNA MACGREGOR

For reminders when new books come out and when backlist titles go on sale, follow her on BookBub @JannaMacGregor, Instagram @jannamacgregor, and join her Facebook group, Janna MacGregor's Lords and Ladies of Langham Hall https://bit.ly/3uGlTHU

Under the Marquess's Mistletoe

EXCERPT

Sleigh Rides and Kisses

Two days before Christmas, 1812
Leyton, just outside of London
Lord and Lady Bentley's Annual Christmas House Party

The joyful jangle of the Christmas bells on the horses' harnesses came to a slow stop before Lady Sophia Rowan. It was the season of romance and her courtship with Lord Tristan Fitz-James, the Earl of Hawkford, had blossomed over the last several months. Most particularly during this house party. Sophia had every expectation that she and Tristan will soon be kissing and touching more deeply and intimately than they've ever been allowed before.

And she could hardly contain her excitement.

It wasn't just because Lord and Lady Bentley relaxed the rules for chaperons guarding young ladies. They did that every year. Sophia had been alone with Tristan before throughout the years. But this time was different. She could feel it. A proposal of marriage might be hers tonight.

This was their first chance to be alone without children screaming joyfully, or adults hovering a little too close. Since she'd arrived at Thorneworth Hall two days ago, Sophia and Tristan had been surrounded by family and friends who greeted them with hugs and laughter and beautiful cheer. But in minutes, they would finally be together without an audience.

"Harrison," Tristan's deep voice called out. "Where have you been? Lady Sophia and I have been waiting for half an hour."

Mr. Jeremy Harrison, who happened to be Sophia's cousin, had on his arm the delightful Lady Elsie Morley, Sophia's best friend and the daughter of their hosts.

"Couldn't be helped, Hawkford. The sleigh suddenly became stuck in the snow." He turned to Elsie. "Isn't that right, Lady Elsie?"

She nodded, but the blond curls escaping her hat and her red swollen lips told another story.

They weren't stuck. How could a sleigh get stuck in the snow? They'd been kissing.

Sophia bit the inside of her cheek. She couldn't blame them, kissing was exactly what she wanted to do with Tristan.

Elsie glanced at Sophia. "Soph, tis true." Then she lowered her voice. "I hope you become stuck in the snow as well," she whispered with a wink. "The moon is beautiful."

The footman in charge of the sleighs for the guests stood nearby, expressionless. But the slight movement of his shoulders betrayed his mirth. A twinkle danced in his eye. Everyone shared high spirits at Christmastide.

The holidays were her favorite time of the year. Sophia had waited practically all year to spend this night with Tristan.

After they said goodbye to Jeremy and Elsie, Tristan turned to her. "Come, my love."

It was the first time he'd ever called her that, and the sound of it sent that familiar longing through her.

He took her hand and helped her into the sleigh. She stole a glance at the footman to see if he'd heard the endearment, but thankfully, he was fetching another fur wrap for their comfort.

"My lord." The footman handed the wrap to Tristan.

"Thank you." Tristan smiled, then turned to Sophia. With tender care, he tucked the fur around Sophia's body. When his gloved hands met her hips, he squeezed gently and caught her gaze. The naughty smile sent her stomach into an endless loop of somersaults. There was definitely kissing in their future if that smile was any indication.

Once Tristan was satisfied that the fur was in position, he climbed into the sleigh. He nodded to the footman, snapped the reins, and then they were off. As Tristan kept his eyes on the path, he reached over and entwined his fingers with hers.

Sophia turned slightly to see his profile. "We're finally alone." Her cheeks felt on fire though it was freezing outside.

How had he grown even more handsome over the past year? A square jaw, angular cheeks, and patrician nose, added to his perfection. She sighed softly.

He caught her staring at him and laughed. "What are you doing?"

"I can't believe we're together again," Sophia said. It felt as if she'd known him forever. She'd watched him over the years as his shoulders broadened and he'd gained height and stature. Now, he was taller than his father, the Marquess of Bridebourne. Tristan wore his black hair at a longer length than was considered fashionable, but to Sophia, the style suited him ideally. When his gaze slid to hers, Sophia took a deep breath at the warmth and hunger in his deep brown eyes. It reminded her of the chocolate that they'd shared every night since they'd arrived. Hot and delectable with the consummate amount of sweetness.

As soon as they rounded the first copse of trees and were out of sight, Tristan took her hand in his and raised it to his lips. "Come closer. I want to hold you." He transferred the reins to his other hand, then placed his arm around Sophia's shoulders and pulled her tight. "Merry Christmas, darling."

"Merry Christmas," she hummed as she rested her head against his shoulder and shared the fur with him. Her heart pounded in rhythm with the clip-clop of the two horses pulling the sleigh. This was going to be their best Christmas together ever.

As soon as they crested the hill, Tristan pulled the sleigh to a stop. Below them, a frozen pond twinkled. The snow glistened from the glow of the new full moon shining down. Multitudes of stars twinkled in the winter night sky.

Tristan took off his gloves, then turned to face her and cupped her cheeks. "Lady Sophia Maria Rowan." Thick and uneven, his voice deepened. "You are every man's dream."

She placed her hands around the neck of his greatcoat. "I don't care about other men. I just want to be one particular man's dream." When Tristan smiled, Sophia pulled him closer. "Because he's my dream."

Slowly, Tristan closed the distance between them. With his thumb, he caressed her lower lip. The muscles of his throat moved as he swallowed. "May I?"

"You don't have to ask. Your kiss is all I've thought about."

"Didn't you think about me?" He leaned in, wearing a wry smile, then angled his mouth to hers.

She closed her eyes and waited for their mouths to meet. When his lips pressed against hers, she became lost in the touch. She wanted to crawl inside his coat and placed her hands on his chest. She craved to explore every inch of him and this irresistible newness between them. She longed to revel in the wonder of Tristan.

But there was a hunger between them that they'd never shared before. As his lips molded to fit hers, Tristan deepened the kiss. His tongue boldly slipped past her lips, and she opened more to allow it.

His body was so different from hers. Through his greatcoat, she could feel the hardness of his chest and his legs. Her soft curves melded to his hard angles. She moaned slightly, wanting more of him. One arm slipped beneath her velvet cloak. His hand skated upward across her gown and corseted ribcage then down. He repeated the soft caresses over and over until he purposely reached her breast. His fingers tightened gently.

His touch sparked a fire within her, the heat consuming her. The need to be closer grew fierce. As she pulled him tighter against her, his kiss instantly gentled.

"Sophia," he whispered as if in pain. "This passion between us is getting stronger." He pressed his lips against hers again. "We were made for each other. I need to ask you a question." He slipped off the bench seat and knelt before her.

Her heart pounded in her chest. This was it. He was going to propose. She swallowed, hoping to find her voice.

"Whoa, there," a male voice called out, interrupting whatever he'd been about to ask.

Not letting go of her hands, Tristian turned simultaneously as she did. Another sleigh was easing to a stop beside them.

"Uncle Patrick and Aunt Martha," she whispered.

"What the deuce are they doing out here?" Tristan mumbled. A practiced smile graced his lips. "Hello," he called out.

Uncle Patrick chuckled while Aunt Martha craned her neck to attain a better glimpse of her and Tristan.

"Merry Christmas," Uncle Patrick proclaimed as he took his wife's hand and brought it to his mouth. "There's nothing more romantic than a winter sleigh ride." He winked in Tristan's direction.

With an athletic grace, Tristan rose from the floor of the sleigh. "Indeed."

"Sophia, your mother wants you to come in from the cold," Aunt Martha said softly with regret in her eyes. "A game of hide and seek is about to start, and Elsie was asking for you."

Uncle Patrick nodded. "You shouldn't miss it." He looked into the sky and pointed. "Likely those clouds will bring more snow. We need it if we're going to have that snowball battle tomorrow." He flicked the reins, and the horses jerked to motion. "We'll see you back at the house."

As the bells of the sleigh jingled off in the distance, Tristan turned and waggled his eyebrows. "I think a game of hide and seek will be perfect."

Sophia was about to argue, but Tristan pressed his lips against hers.

"Meet me in our special place beneath the entry hall stairs. We'll hide there." His eyes smoldered in promise. "We can kiss to our heart's content without anyone being the wiser."

Ready for more of Sophia and Tristan?
https://amzn.to/3PzgqOu

Read on for a preview of the next exciting book in the Scoundrels and Scandals of Drury Lane, The Duchess of Drury Lane

by
Janna MacGregor.

For the latest news and freebies from Janna, sign up for her Newsletter.

Visit https://www.jannamacgregor.com for more information about Janna's books.

Connect with Janna MacGregor Online
Twitter
Facebook
Ladies of Langham Hall Facebook Group
Instagram
BookBub
Sign Up for the Newsletter

Read The Cavensham Heiresses Series

The Bad Luck Bride
The Bride Who Got Lucky
The Luck of the Bride
The Good, The Bad, and The Duke
Rogue Most Wanted
Wild, Wild Rake

Read The Widow Rules Series

UNDER THE MARQUESS'S MISTLETOE

Where There's a Will
A Duke in Time
Rules for Engaging the Earl

Mistletoe Christmas with Eloisa James, Christi Caldwell, Janna MacGregor, and Erica Ridley

For the latest news and freebies from Janna, sign up for her Newsletter.

Visit https://www.jannamacgregor.com for more information about Janna's books.

The Duchess of Drury Lane

Read on for a preview of the next exciting book in the Scoundrels and Scandals of Drury Lane, <u>The Duchess of Drury Lane</u>
by
Janna MacGregor.

Drury Lane
London

Chapter One

For most theatre lovers, the opportunity to have a private tour of Drury Lane would definitely be preferable to having a tooth pulled. However, this was not the case for Miss Celeste Worsley, who stood outside the noble theatre alongside Alice Cummings.

If Celeste's grandfather found out that Alice was carrying

a baby, he'd have her thrown into the street before Celeste could utter a word in her maid's defense.

Since the first day she'd stepped into her grandfather's house, he had repeatedly warned Celeste that under no circumstances could she bring scandal, dishonor, or embarrassment to the family name.

Yet, two simple words, such as "I'm carrying," foretold a drama that would rival a new play in Drury Lane. Celeste would do everything in her power to protect Alice from her grandfather, and anyone else who might humiliate her maid. The truth was that Alice wasn't just a lady's maid. She was Celeste's friend and had been ever since Celeste's mother had first employed her.

"Alice, how did this happen?" Celeste bit her tongue to keep from cursing. Alice's stomach had become fuller, but Celeste had attributed it to the fact that she always asked her friend to share breakfast with her in her bedroom. It had been a godsend when Alice had agreed. It meant she didn't have to face her grandfather's inquisition about her friends or her parents' letters.

The maid's plump cheeks blossomed into a color that would make poppies jealous. "Well, Miss, you know about the birds and the bees. Not to mention his and her bits and how they fit together."

Celeste lifted her palm. "That's not what I meant. How did you and Benjamin...er...find the time and place?"

Alice chuckled. "That's easily explained. Benjamin's employer, Mr. Hollandale—"

"Wait, for goodness' sake," Celeste hissed. "*Mr. Malcolm Hollandale?*"

Alice nodded. "He's such a nice man."

Celeste couldn't attest to his pleasant personality. She'd barely said two words to the man, but she had studied him at every society event they attended together. It wasn't an exaggeration to say that she was an expert on his stunningly handsome good looks, the impeccably tailored evening clothes he wore, and how the skin around his captivating sapphire eyes crinkled when he laughed. Tall, blond, and ruggedly gorgeous described him perfectly.

Most of the *ton* considered him the perfect male specimen. But they refused to overlook one simple fact. He was not an aristocrat nor a member of the landed gentry. He was a man of trade. He might be a self-made millionaire and a member of the Duke of Pelham's rarified Millionaires Club, but those facts didn't change anyone's haughty opinion regarding the man.

But Celeste had never cared a whit about that, nor had her heart. It tumbled anew into infatuation every time she saw him. But she had warned that traitorous organ repeatedly—it could gaze to its *heart's content,* but there was to be no engagement.

Alice nodded as if she was privy to Celeste's private thoughts. "Mr. Hollandale allows us to visit in Benjamin's rooms whenever we have time together. They are over Mr. Hollandale's laboratory." She shrugged with a sheepish smile. "We might have gotten a bit enthusiastic during a few of our visits."

"I see," Celeste said. Enthusiastic was an understatement. She patted her maid's arm. "No matter what comes from our conversation today, I'll help you find a way to be with your Benjamin."

"If he doesn't marry me, I'll be ruined." Her maid's throat bobbed when she swallowed, the movement betraying her fear. "I can't go home, Miss. My mam will disown me."

"It won't come to that. Everything you've told me about your Benjamin leads me to believe he'll welcome you and the baby." Several inches taller than her maid, Celeste bent her knees until her gaze met Alice's teary brown eyes. "Trust me?"

When Alice nodded, Celeste took her maid's hand and tugged her up the front steps. "Why is Benjamin here today?"

"Mr. Hollandale's experiment failed, so they must remove it."

Celeste stilled. "They?"

"Ben and Mr. Hollandale," Alice offered.

Celeste hardened her stomach. No matter what happened, her first and only concern was for Alice and her baby. She could not...would not...spend her precious time mooning over Malcolm Hollandale.

It made little difference that every part of her body seemed to tingle when she looked at him.

Without wasting another second, Celeste opened the theatre door and escorted Alice inside. As soon as they stepped into the main auditorium, it appeared that they'd entered a busy beehive. Workers milled around the stage while the pounding of hammers echoed throughout the theatre. A man shouted directions as he pointed at a drawing in his hands.

But none of it caught Celeste's interest. Her eyes were focused on Malcolm Hollandale, the bane of her existence. It wasn't that he was rude or ignored her. Quite the opposite. Whenever she'd seen him at a *ton* event, he had been most courteous to her and everyone else. But Celeste couldn't concentrate on anything or anyone else when he was in the room. Consequently, men thought her standoffish. She wasn't. She was simply under Malcolm Hollandale's spell. Thankfully, he had no idea about her true feelings.

She'd be horrified if he ever discovered that she was totally and irrevocably in love with him. That proved her heart hadn't listened to any of her warnings about looking but not engaging.

Alice bounced on her toes as she raised her hand in a wave. All Celeste's attention was focused on Malcolm Hollandale, but then a man on his hands and knees stood and waved back.

THE DUCHESS OF DRURY LANE

Celeste bent her head and released a deep breath. She had to get ahold of herself. Alice wasn't waving at Hollandale. She was waving at the young man working next to him, who must be Benjamin. Celeste would do well to remember that the world didn't revolve around Mr. Hollandale.

Benjamin said something to Malcolm, who nodded. As Alice's beau approached them, Celeste stood still like a rabbit caught by a fox's penetrating stare. Malcolm's eyes were locked on hers for a moment that surely lasted an hour. What kind of a man who was graced by the gods' own hands and looked like Apollo worked as a common laborer?

A very real, but very sweaty Malcolm Hollandale.

Her cheeks grew unbearably hot, but she refused to turn away. Her grandfather was the Duke of Exehill. It was one of the oldest titles in the British Isles, and she'd always been taught never to lower her gaze to anyone.

And that included a devilishly handsome man who made her heartbeat accelerate faster than a thoroughbred at the Royal Ascot. She should know fast horses. Her father bred and sold them to peers, their heirs, other sons, and anyone else who was mad about the creatures.

Hollandale smirked when she'd lifted her chin. Without second-guessing her cause, she marched straight toward him. If her plan had any hopes of succeeding, she needed Malcolm Hollandale's help.

And Malcolm Hollandale needed her.

He just didn't know it yet.

* * * *

On his hands and knees scrubbing away his latest attempt at creating a hardwood floor varnish, Malcolm Hollandale didn't know whether he was more frustrated that his failed varnish had turned into a sticky mess or the fact that he was sweating as if he were attending a smithy's fire.

"Ack, Hollandale, I'm sorry I had to ask you to remove it."

Florizel Holland, the theatre's stage manager, scratched his head as he grimaced at the floor. "If this exact spot weren't where we mark the actor's positions for tonight's performance, I would tell you to leave it until the new production begins." He shrugged.

Malcolm stopped. "Thank you, but that would be too dangerous. If one of your actors stepped in this exact spot, I'm afraid they'd be stuck until the final curtain."

"It might help a few of them. Some of the actors don't know how to stand still when they deliver their lines." Florizel smiled. "I appreciate you coming so quickly. If you continue sanding at that speed, we will not have to miss rehearsal today."

"Florizel," someone called.

"You're popular today," Malcolm quipped.

"I always am when there are problems." Florizel nodded at the understudy who called him. "I'll bid you farewell."

"Mr. Hollandale?" Benjamin Brannan stopped his work and sat on his haunches. He pointed at two women. "It's my Alice. She's been feeling poorly lately." He turned and waved at her. "May I—"

"Go," Malcolm said, not wasting a second. "I'm the one who created this mess. I should be the one to clean it."

"Thank you, sir," Benjamin said as he rose to his feet.

Malcolm smiled at the young man. Ben had been working beside Malcolm for nearly two years and was one of the hardest-working employees Malcolm had ever had the good fortune to hire. So, whenever Benjamin asked for a break, Malcolm never refused him.

He continued to sand away on the floor but slowed his motion when he noticed Celeste Worsley's fragrance wafting in the air around him, which was amazing since the entire theatre could host over three-thousand-six-hundred visitors at a time. Yet even in such a cavernous space, he knew the exact moment she'd entered the building.

She stood back from the stage and seemed to be comforting Alice, the lady's maid whom Benjamin had taken a fancy to. Ben and Alice were from the same small town. Malcolm would wager that the two of them would marry if Alice could be convinced to give up her position as Celeste Worsley's maid.

Malcolm had met Miss Celeste Worsley over a year ago at a *ton* event. Even though she was the very definition of an incomparable beauty who possessed excellent poise and deportment, he always detected censure in her gaze when she looked upon him. For some unknown reason, she'd taken an instant dislike to him and had never bothered to hide her contempt. She always smirked, although slightly, whenever she glanced in his direction.

As Malcolm stole a peek, he sighed. She wore her typical expression of disapproval.

It aggravated him to no end. Her parents were the definition of scandal. He'd wager that their daughter was on a first-name basis with scandalous behavior. The apple never falls far from the tree and all that. He wiped the sweat out of his eyes. For God's sake, he was one of the rare millionaires of Mayfair. Alas, there were only a select few peers he considered friends. Though, his friends had no trouble accepting him for who he was, an inventor with impeccable manners. They were the rare exception. Most people could not ignore his humble upbringing despite his wealth.

Including Celeste Worsley. Though a mere viscount's daughter, she walked and talked as if she were a duchess in her own right. He chuckled, wondering what she'd think of the moniker he'd given her. She'd likely scowl even more if she knew that he called her the Duchess of Drury Lane.

As he continued to sand the sticky varnish from the floor,

Malcolm stole another glance in her direction. He slowed the repetitive sanding motion while tracking her movements but leaned his weight into the work.

As Celeste held her head high, she walked as if she indeed were a duchess. If it were anyone else, he'd smile in welcome, but it was Celeste Worsley in all her judgmental glory. Even if she did think she was better than any other human, he couldn't deny that watching her was one of his favorite pastimes.

He returned to staring at his hands but knew the moment when she was before the stage. Less than ten feet separated them.

"Mr. Hollandale? I wonder if I might have a word with you."

Her sweet voice twisted itself around his chest and squeezed like a clinging vine, robbing him of breath. For the love of heaven, even his cock took notice and twitched at the sound. How could a woman such as she cause all his logic and intelligence to take its leave?

"Mr. Hollandale?" she repeated.

This time at the sound of his name, he pushed all of his weight into the sandpaper. That's when he heard the sound of the wood creaking and cracking beneath him.

"Mr. Hollandale, you're bleeding."

He looked down to see a splinter the size of a one-hundred-year-old elm stuck in the middle of his palm. It didn't register what was happening until the excruciating throbbing struck him with the force of a hurricane.

"*Bloody hell!*" Pure instinct drove Malcolm to shake his hand as if that would dislodge the offending tree. Blood trailed down his arm. He pulled his hand to his chest. For a moment, he was afraid he would cast up his accounts from the pain.

"Let me help."

When he looked up, he couldn't believe the sight before

him. Somehow, Celeste had climbed onto the stage and reached for his hand.

"There's no need," he said brusquely.

"There's every need," she said, not paying a whit of attention to his curtness. "You're bleeding, and I have a clean handkerchief at my disposal.

Like a wounded animal, he flinched when she reached for his hand.

"I have suffered splinters myself. They can become quite nasty if you don't clean the wound and dig out the irritating piece of wood." Instead of chiding him for acting like a child, she soothed him. "Do you suppose there's any brandy around?" She laughed. "What am I saying? There must be. This is a theatre, after all. Actors are notorious for insisting upon only serving the finest brandy in such an establishment." She leaned close and lowered her voice. "I dare say that you and I could use a little tipple ourselves after this day. Come with me."

Tipple? What lady of good breeding used that term?

Who was this woman standing before him, and what had she done with the incredibly proper and enormously conceited Celeste Worsley?

Want to read more? Pick up The Duchess Of Drury Lane at all your favorite retailers here:

https://books2read.com/u/mK7Axv

For more information about Janna's books and the latest news and freebies, sign up for her newsletter at https://www.jannamacgregor.com.

Made in the USA
Monee, IL
23 April 2024